BACK TO BACK

BY BENJAMIN BENSON SINGH BHAMRA

Published in 2017 by FeedARead.com Publishing

First Edition

A CIP catalogue record for this title is available from the British Library.

BACK TO BACK
BY BENJAMIN BENSON SINGH BHAMRA

INTRODUCTION

It was a time of peace 300 hundred years after the last war, I had been frozen for a war crime 300 years ago 2020 the year now was 2320 I was being woken from a deep freeze, I did not know who I was and the company were not going to tell me it was by the company I did not know that I was their target they needed to wake me as there was something in my body that they wanted. They were after a microchip, which contained accident war plans they wanted to kill me so they could move around the legal plans and the side of things. So, they sent me a girl, she was part of the set up. As she had the second part of the chip. Once the chips were together they would hold the plans or war. The company wanted war every country, every race, children, adults and teenagers the whole planet the company wanted war. I was put there to stop them, my name is Benjamin.

PREFACE

This story is based on the word peace and a little bit of war I want the reader to believe in the future rather than the past. There are lots and lots of action it is based on the concerns of the planet as it stands but not in 2320 that is all make believe. In my imagination, it would or could probably happen. I know I'm making myself sound like a war monger but it is quite the opposite. It is a pledge for peace and the world in Benjamin's eyes. As his mind has changed after 3000 years of sleep. He has the plans for war trapped in his eye in a microchip and the bad guys want it back this will take you on a roller-coaster of a ride and an adventure as Benjamin escapes and escapes from the company who want him dead for the chip.

CHAPTER ONE
BACK TO BACK

It was a time of peace and it all started with the girl her name was Lucy she was walking through one of the city's parks but she had no idea what was going to happen, it was late about twelve o'clock. I could not tell you exactly what the year was, I had just woken up from a deep freeze. My name was Benjamin I was aa space detective or in better terms a cybercop. I had been sent by the company to retrieve and watch the girl. The girl was going to pick something up I was there to receive it, it was my job. I was close to her but not close enough. It started in a second there was a man running through the park I knew about this as I had visualized it while I was in the deepfreeze. He was being chased by some bad people I do not know what they called themselves just yet. From nowhere there was a space ship it had landed within seconds. Two aliens got out they had big guns and looks weird, they were not human. I do know what they were called I was watching there was a man he was running it looked like he bumped into her knocking her onto the floor on purpose and leaving the microchip in her pocket the aliens did not see and continued after the man a chase had started I was on an ear piece waiting for conformation to engage. The company never got back to me.
The man who was fleeing was fast but the alien men were faster within a couple of seconds they had him in fire range and within a couple more seconds they he was dead. They checked his body for the microchip but it was not on him but now on the girl. It was my chance to grab her Lucy, as I did they had turned around and had made us their new targets I grabbed the girl by the arm speaking to her giving her the low down as she put up a fight it was obvious that she was reluctant to come with me. as she struggled even more as I pulled her arm. Trying to stop her from screaming and shouting. As she continued I pulled her through the oak walking fast towards my space car and out of the entrance of the park she finally caught on after I yelled at her and shouted you should come with me if you do not want

to die. I answered the question for her. Then she spoke "No" I replied "exactly". I had answered her. I continued
"If you do not come with me we will be both mincemeat".
She decided to comply in the end.
"where are you taking me ". She said in a childlike snotty attitude girl like.
"I have a friend close by we can go there until we are out of danger.
The girl did not answer then she answered. The spoke it was like she had woke up a totally different person she started "what's going on who were those aliens and who was the man and why did they kill him".
I replied "I cannot tell you I do not know I am surprised as you. However, you have something that I need ".
"what I do not know you and we have never5 met before I do not recall ".
"not right now but in the future, you have nothing to worry about I am on your side".

"on my side on my side on my side of what "
"Look lady I have just been released from prison and the last thing I want to do is to go back if you…. Forget it". the car is just around the corner.
"where are you taking me ".
Benjamin does not answer they make to the car they both get in. "They are still following us I can feel them".
"Oh, you have special powers as well ".
Benjamin looks at her she laughs.
She then knocks herself out on Benjamin's dash board with all the excitement. Benjamin looks onwards but the girl out cold all he can do is comfort her. Benjamin sits tight waiting for thebaines to make a move from the area he opens his window for some fresh air and a better view as he does their space ship fly's over them and moves in a northern direction and leaves the scene.
Before they had a chance to think I could sense a feeling thtbthe had not left the scene completely infect they had not left the scene I was right they were close, closer than I could think. They had not left the area. I closed my eyes to see what I could see what I could see it was a gift that bi had and I had it from when I was a child I had received it from my first death and my first life there was nothing I tried and tried

again but nothing. I presumed that me and the girl Lucy were out of danger. But I was wrong just as I was about to leave I could hear them they were closer than I thought. I pushed the ignition button in the car and drove away fast. As I took the first corner they were there as I took the first corner they had been waiting for me they unleash a mass of gun fire. Destroying everything around us. I yelled to the computer in my car shields they went up only for a minute. The computer was telling me that there was a malfunction, the girl was just waking up. I smashed the computer yelling out shields in desperation. As I sat there in the driver's seat pushing the touch button ignition forgetting that it was voice activated.

The car engine started we were out of there I was not a happy bunny.
"What did I miss ". The girl says as she awakes.
I replied "a lot of action ".
Benjamin gets away and head s for one of his friends' houses. In all the hell fire Benjamin's radio is down he can no longer communicate with his team. As Benjamin pulls up into the drive way he senses that there is something wrong he closes his eyes to see if he cans see the future.
Again, he sees nothing and get nothing he steps out of the car and tells the girl to hurry up. She again gets out the car in a snotty huff. And continues to ask questions all over again. Benjamin replies with an anionic "shut up".
She does saluting him as she walks around the car. She upsets Benjamin again he grabs her by the arm and pulls her towards the house Benjamin walks toward s the house dragging her behind him. Benjamin knocks on the door their silence for a moment Benjamin try's his ear piece not sure where his team is. As he contacts them there is nothing again. As he slowly takes his fingers off the ear piece he knocks on the door again.

Benjamin still believes that there is something wrong the girl pushes the door open "it's open 2. She says
"what is ". Benjamin reply's.
The girl Lucy was just about to walk in. Benjamin sticks out his arm shutting her backwards the girl angel pushes his arm off her.
"what she says "angry and frustrated.
"just wait "Benjamin insists.
"what is it" she whispers.

A few minutes later Benjamin tells her to go in, in front of him she walks in in front of him. Into the hall way. Benjamin walks in after her as she walks in she was just about to shout if there was anybody there but however on this occasion she realizes what she was about to do she hold s her tongue, and then Benjamin says to her quietly "be quiet". She understands. He tells her to keep walking. Then on purpose she shouts "is there anybody there ".
Benjamin grabs her quickly taking both her arms and quickly and calmly pulls aside and speaks to her.
"Do you want to end up dead". There was no answer. Benjamin finds the main reception room that is the living room. They both walk in there in the room in front of them is a man he is sitting down on the sofa he was dead.
"he is dead".
"I know I'm not blind ".
She continues "you dragged me all this way to see this ".
"yeah well, your luckily it could be you, search him".
"No". she replied.
"I said search him"

"Who is he, he must have some credentials all I was given was this address".
"He was our way out of here".
Benjamin takes a step backwards not knowing that his killer was behind him all he hears is the kellick of a gun then he knows. Then a voice.
"It's a forty-five I'll ask the question you just answer them".
The girl Lucy try's to but in, he warns to stay quiet and tells her to sit down.

She sits down and within a minute she is telling the bad guy everything she starts to talk hoping that Benjamin catches on. As it was supposed to be a distraction. She continues,
"look I have been fired and I have been dragged from place to place to place, I have been kidnapped and now I have been introduced to a dead guy. I am not a happy person and I have had a really bad day".
Benjamin joins in.

It's true she has. Benjamin catches on quickly. The gun was behind Benjamin he clicks the gun pulling a bullet in to the gun chamber. She continues "I AM HAVING A REALLY BAD DAY". The gun man seems to weaken as the Lucy continues her plan seems to be working. Benjamin could see that she was not a fool and her plans were working he knew that she was faking it. as this was happening the gun man was asking her about the microchip. She continued. "What microchip I do not know what are you talking about".
The conversation was just enough to put the gun man off Benjamin for a second. Benjamin steps backward for a moment resting his head on the gun as the gun is pointing at the back of his head. Knowing that the gun was close enough to him to make a maunder. As quick as lightening he turns around the gun was now pointing at his face he quickly removes the gun from his face and the man's hands. As he does the girl is trying to remove herself and is trying to get out of the way. The microchip falls out of her dress onto the floor as she looks for the chip she gets involved in Benjamin fight with the man. As Benjamin falls backwards over her he shouts out" hay". Then again shouting "get out of the way".
Benjamin shouts as he plants another punch onto the man's face. as he clasps the gun both hands on Benjamin stands on the chip as they are still struggling. Just as the girl was going to pick it up the bad guy stands on it he does not know then he moves his foot but then Benjamin stands on it he does not know either as he is busy trying to fight the man, Benjamin punches him again while he was getting a punch or two himself. Benjamin falls over the girl it was not over yet. The who was under Benjamin's feet falls back on to the settee on to the dead man's lap. Who is still in his seat.

The fight continues the man jumps on Benjamin again Benjamin throws him off this time he drops his gun. The girl picks it up, and then finds the chip on the floor Lucy was about to pick it up just as she reaches for it the treads on it again then kicks across the room not knowing of course. As Benjamin hits the deck again the man turns to Lucy it was her turn next. He grabs her throwing her across the room she screams as she gets up off the floor, she shouts for Benjamin who was just getting up, rubbing his face Benjamin looks around for something to hit the man with he finds a bottle but before he has a chance to grab it the man does smashing the bottle on to Benjamin's head. The bottle did not break and Benjamin stands there surprised. They start to struggle again as Benjamin must disarm him the, the girl takes is a swipe at the man but hits Benjamin instead. Benjamin eyes start to sting as the bottle had a something in it and whatever was in it went into Benjamin's eyes. Benjamin cry's out the girl does not know what to do. Benjamin shouts out again "I'm blind." Benjamin is now acting crazy and his eyes are burning, Benjamin is now in the dark in pain. But because he has special vision. As the man gets up off the floor were Benjamin had put Benjamin leaches a massive kung Fu attack.

CHAPTER TWO

"Is he dead" the girl asks.
"I've broken his neck" Benjamin replies as he starts to check the body over. The man was wearing a black suit, Benjamin turns out his pockets but nothing he had nothing on him to say who he was or where he came from. He checks again just to double check this time he finds s a wallet.
Benjamin continues as he looks inside "no nothing".
He continues without being interrupted by the girl "who the hell are these people, I mean are they serious, space ships, bullet proof cars, and now I have murdered somebody."
The girl Lucy does not answer she was still in shock for a moment then she was looking for an answer but before she can explain her self-Benjamin hears something.
"there somebody here ". Benjamin tells the girl to be quiet.
He continues "there's something going on outside can you hear it ". He whispers.
The sound was getting louder and louder he insist that they leave the building quickly. not Forgetting about the chip. The girl wants to hand it over but Benjamin does not give her a chance. As they were now on the run again. As they make their way up stairs the company was there, Benjamin and the Lucy head straight for their car. The girl is shouting as Benjamin pushes her into the passage seat telling her to be quiet, he jumps in on the other side.
He switches his computer on "which is the fastest and quickest way out of here". He asks.
He then finishes the conversation with "we need a place to blend in". He turns on the engine and continues "blend in like a camellia." In all the excitement, he gets an answer from his computer "the nearest place is town according to this map."
"right can you take me there."
As the computer takes control of the car and heads off there was a couple of loud shots, Benjamin believe that they were just warning shots just to let him know that they were close and the game of

running was not over yet. The car drives of with the computer listening to the girl but the girl gets it wrong she continues.
"where are we this is not right."
Benjamin answers her "what do you mean are you reading the map correctly."
She says, "it's upside down instead of moving away further from them we are moving closer."

Benjamin hits the breaks and with a U-turn now they were heading in the right direction as they drive they knew that they were being followed. The company's space ships fly past them and over them at a super speed.
"we have them again captain."
"Good this time finish the job and get me the microchip."

"We are being followed."
"I gathered that." Was Benjamin's reply.
"then put your foot down." She says
"It's down pork chop."
"Knock it off with the compliments."
Benjamin drives extremely fast and while driving is giving the girl Lucy the low down telling her where they were going as he tells her that they are heading into town Benjamin continues to tell her that they might be able with a bit of luck and lose them in town Benjamin puts his foot down again.
"I think we have lost them." Lucy says.
"I do not think so I do not seem or feel safe." Benjamin says that they were still about them he says that he could feel there presents it was like that they were right in front him, this vision that he was having it was like he could touch them.
Out of the blue the girls kick off starting an argument.
"what the hell do you want."
"They want the microchip you have it in your hiding in your dress I saw you and I saw what that man in the park did".
The girl tries to lie at first pretending that nothing had happened Benjamin implies that if she was lying it will get her nowhere.

She bows down in the end.
“so that’s what this is all about.”
Benjamin decides to fill her in but does not tell her the full story or what the microchip is for. But tells her that it is important enough to bring him out of his death into a new life and as he tries to explain that he was frozen in the past so he could enter the future so he could access the chip he continues to explain but does not tell enough as he did not trust her.

The girl agreed but started to ask questions what did it have to do with her Benjamin reply's that he saw everything that had happened in the park still not realia=zing that Lucy the girl was all part of the set up. He continues and tells her that he saw the guy bump into and slip her the chip as he was running for his life which ended in his death. The girl insists in asking who was the man. I did not know for sure as he had only been on the planet for a short while. All I know is that I was ordered to receive the chip and send it back to the company. For some strange reason, he planted it on you. The girl wanted out Benjamin tells her that she cannot let her go as for one it was too dangerous and for two she had to return the chip. The girls reply to was a sad one as she had the chip she undoes her dress and takes it out of her bra. Benjamin thanks her for being honest Benjamin believes that his job is done and asks the girl to celebrate with him they fly further into town to find a restaurant to eat at. As they fly there he asks the girl hungry. Benjamin and the girl Lucy asks for the menu and start ordering. Benjamin and Lucy are hitting it off and getting on. The girl was drunk and beaming knew that they were still being followed as the girl was getting more and more noisy the restaurant was filling there was celebration happening there was camera men everywhere. But that was soon the change as Benjamin was watching his back as well as the girls. As he pours the girl anther drink and looks up at the celling the roof is vibrating Benjamin realities that again there was something wrong they had been found.

"there's something wrong."

The girl was drunk and did not answer, and when she Didi as she had consumed so much her drunken answer was a shored

"I do not care leave me behind."

I was trying hard to get the message to her all she could say was leave me then "what."

Trying not to make too much of the scene I told her again. Benjamin noticed the trembling on the celling again he was taking no chances, he grabs the by her hand just in time pulling her through many photographers. The celling really shaking as they left.

"come on this way we have company again." Benjamin says.

Benjamin pulls her by her hand and takes the lead, as they just get to the entrance there a small explosion smashing the restaurants windows but only the windows. There was a rush to the doors all the people

including the press were shouting as Benjamin and Lucy turned to look at what was left all they could see was dead people. There was body's everywhere. Then he hears a voice.
"would you like me to hit the pause button Benjamin."
"It continued "give me the girl and the microchip, it can be arranged."
The bad guys had found them Benjamin pulls the girl behind to protect her. He voices starts again and this time Benjamin is trying to find where it was coming from.
"Come on Benjamin what's worth more your life or that little bit of the future just think all the live s we can save., I'm sure that you do not another war on your conscious."

Benjamin does not answer in accordance to a ray of bullets and more gun fire which the company spread through the room. Benjamin decides to run again he grabs the girl who was still drunk and they both run not out of the restaurant but further into it. they dash to the kitchen there's was more gun fire pots and pans and all kind s of kitchen stuff being blow up and bullets imbedding the walls they outside, beaming closes his eye and visualizes the escape, he shouts to the Lucy upstairs they make it to the roof there was helicopter right in front them Benjamin throws the piolet out and pushes the girl in and says great fully.
"it was probably that rich guy down stairs he will not mind his dead."
The girl steps out of the helicopter as Benjamin gets in he must go and receive her she was picking up Benjamin grabs and pushes her back in to the helicopter. Benjamin knows that within a minute they will have company again he shots frantically as he is looking for something to jam the stairs well doors. it would give him the extra minute to warm the helicopter up for their escape. He eventually finds s a piece of wire and his credit card. As he lodges the cards into the door, then quickly tied the door shut. The girl is still drunk and tell him to take it up.
"who's flying this baby." She insists that she should. Benjamin did not have a clue and in a hurry decided that if she said that she could fly it then she could they swap seats quickly. As Benjamin and the Lucy swap places so that she could take control the company's men are just about to make an appearance. The helicopter was finally ready Lucy take s the helicopter up.
As the company's men break the door open there was an array of gun fire one of the men had a rocket launcher as Benjamin tells the girl to

take them higher it ws too late the bad guys had launched the missile it hit the tail taking Benjamin and Lucy out. They were now plummeting fast back to the ground. There was no explosion and Benjamin thinks that they may have missed and it was the lucks flying except it was a side winder and it was coming back straight to them the missile hits them ripping off the tail and sending them back to the ground the girls control was incredible she managed to land it without killing the both of us. We are down. Benjamin tells to get out of the chopper as there was another missile heading on its way. They had a snipper also.
"Yeah ha" he shouts as he unleashes an array of bullets one after another Benjamin does not know and keeps walking in and out of the guns scope. The second missile finally hits the helicopter and destroy the company believes that they had won but in fact they had lost gain on this occasion the snipper and the man with the rocket launcher pull away and head down stairs the assess the damage. Benjamin and Lucy do a U-turn after a quick bark watching the flames of the helicopter for a moment and thanking each other. They got back into the game going back to the restaurant so they can get the car and make another get away as Lucy ducks in and out of there sight Benjamin slips past a few of them opening the car quietly and calmly waits for Lucy.
"So, what now." the girl asks.
"I guess if they think that we are dead we can go home." Benjamin replies.
"I can go home good."
The girl was kind of getting upset and I already knew that she was temperamental. The girl asks Benjamin if she could have a lift home and Benjamin agrees and they make tracks Benjamin always hated good byes he could just about get his head around her the girl steps upon her porch the dim light just giving her the light she needed to kiss him good bye and wish him good night. Benjamin turns around and bleeps his car doors to unlock. He parks his car a little bit further down the drive way he knows that it was not over yet just to see if his theory about the girl is right.
Benjamin falls back to sleep he is gifted with the sight of vision he could see things that on other person could see he see into minds and he was watching her through his. I suppose you could call it x-ray vision, night vision and infer red vision all in the same place waiting for me to turn it on.
He was watching her this time she was in the shower it was good to have these special, super powers except they had their curses. After I

had stopped watching her I had decided that she was safe. I pushed the ignition on the dash and drove off in to the night as I drove further down the road I had the feeling that something was not right I thought for a split second that it was me and just me and I needed a break from all the action which had happened in the last couple of days. It had worn me out but it was not to be. Benjamin pulls over for some petrol. As he parks his car and is filling her up. As he walks into the the shop and towards the counter not really taking much notice another car pulls up. Out of the corner of his eye he sees a man he is dressed in black he knew straight away it was a hit man he told himself to be cool but it was too late. Within a second the attendant was dead two bullets to the chest straight through the window Benjamin draws his weapon handing it from site the hit man takes his time
"I guess you're just in the wrong place at the wrong time"
He picks up a can of beer and opens it as he takes is a mouth full and tosses the can aside.
He then picks up another can be drinking it all straight down.
Benjamin is hesitating to watch carefully and speaking to himself he did not ask him straight out but he wanted to know his name.
Benjamin reaches for a can the hitman seemed to think that it was fair What the hitman did not know was beaming was going to throw the can and put a bullet in it to shunt his vision as he does he then goes for his gun the hitman being blinded but only for a moment leaving Benjamin in the position to fire upon him the plan worked the man was dead Benjamin rolls him over he does not recognise him.
Benjamin makes it back to his car but not before he questions the dying man.
"who sent you"
There was no answer.
Benjamin finishes him off.
Benjamin wants to know who else is following that man was not dressed like the company.
However, the man on the floor ws not dead as I went to turn my ignition he just rose up probably adrenaline he went for his gun I yelled out shields the computer switched very fast an array of built hit my window screen I hit the push the ignition button as I did the car engine was on I drove straight at him as I mashed into him trapping him between petrol station wall and the bonnet of the car, this time I had to make sure I carefully approached him. pulling him by his hair and watching the pour out of his mouth on the bonnet of my car

questioned him again and again I got nothing this time I'm putting you asleep for good I raised my gun forcing it into the side of his head and pulled the trigger.

CHAPTER THREE

As Benjamin reversed to free him it was clear that he had left him with a couple of bullet holes and a pair of broken legs. Benjamin walks over to the body again kicking his silencer aside Benjamin kicks the gun further away again. He was bleeding through his mouth the accident must have forced him to bite his own tongue off or in half. I looked at him I knew those eyes and they were telling me to finish it. Benjamin pulls the gun out of his jacket and points at the man. He was clearly dead already Benjamin refuses to take it any farther than that. He turns and walks away leaving the dead man on the floor. As Benjamin gets into his car he sees from a distant that he Didi nave some commutation with him it was the phone it ws lying about twenty feet from him Benjamin jumps out theca quickly as now he could hear the sirens he picks it up puts it in to his jacket and drives off. Town minutes down the road the phone rings he pulls over ken owing that he had not a lot of time and answers it. knowing what Benjamin had heard the hit had nothing to do with him he turns the phone off and throws it out of the car window. I was in the wrong place at the wrong time he recalls the gentle man's words. Benjamin was now speaking to himself.
"Why." He says to himself
He could hear the echoes of the man that he had just killed and the word she was saying.
"You were in the wrong place at the wrong time."
Taking in to mind that the man was going to kill me rather him than me. Benjamin preaches for a moment he believed that it was not his fault. He considers the rear-view mirror and find s out that he was being followed by the police they got close close enough to pull him over it was just his luck but then as he was on the side of the road the police car just past him by. There must have been an emergency somewhere else.

"few that was lucky."
The computer then replies, "you are running out of fuel."
My computer was acting up again. He continues to talk to his computer.
"it is about time you told me who you are, look I'm fed up with playing this game."
Benjamin turns off the ignition as he ungrasps the steering wheel.
Computer tells him.
"I cannot tell you what I do not know."
All I was trying to do was to find the microchip which I have and so I was watching you and following you. The computer continues.
"these people do not mess around if they want you dead you are dead and until they get the microchip I cannot go home and you cannot either.
"Right now, my communications are down.
And right now, I'm telling you that those space being are right behind you so I am going to have to guess your only escape is me so buckle up sit back and enjoy the journey.

"What about those two dead guys are they part of the game was in on your stupid deal where they part of this game."
"Yes, correct they were part of the game they worked for our boss."
Benjamin was just about to push a button in the car to change it back to manual but the computer butts in.
"I'm driving, this time it is my turn." The computer insists.
"Where are we going." Benjamin asks.
"Silly question really." The computer says in reply
Benjamin is tired and wants to sleep as he closes his eyes and slowly drops off. He does not feel safe with the computer and thinks that his being double crossed. When Benjamin awakes there in the middle of nowhere Benjamin asks why are they at this destination the computer answers him and tells him it a safe place nobody can find us here. Benjamin is thinking as he still feels uncertain, after a couple more hours of sleep Benjamin awakes and turns the computer off. He wants to go home so he takes control again it would probably take him few hours.
As Benjamin was just about to drive off somebody the girl gets into his car he jumps with surprise its Lucy do not ask any questions I

cannot tell what I do not know now get us out of here Benjamin was surprised he smiles and calls the computer an old dog. All I was told ws that I had to receive the microchip do you have it. Benjamin does not answer.
“I have been watching you, following you.” She said.
Benjamin presses the ignition button and they drive away,
“where are we going to” she says then pauses for a minute. “was that a silly question.”
Benjamin starts dreaming there was something about the girl she made him feel peaceful.
He ws dreaming of the past way into the past he was somewhere in the country side he is looking at the trees and then he wakes up. He keeps the dream to himself and he knows that it is recurring as he has had it before. He does not understand it yet. When Benjamin awakes he wakes up in shock he grabs the dashboard. Then unconsciously lashes out. Nobody says anything. He snows awake with the girl in the car by his side. The girl is in the back seat. And had left the car on autopilot a bird lands on the wing mirror as he wakes again he words wryer no more, no more dreams. The girl not really taking any notice of what he had said jumps into the passages seat.
She talkative and believes that she is helping wake up. Stupidly she turns on the radio, he in reply to her actions turns it off.
“no music.”
“this is not a celebration this is my home.”
The car pulls up into the drive way, the computer in the car turns everything off but only after it re connects its self to the houses system. The computer wakes Benjamin by telling him that they had reached their destination.

The girl gets out of the car Benjamin follows her she calls out feeling excited.
“have you got the keys.”
“Computer open the door and turn on all the lights.” Benjamin speaks.
“It has recognition, nice.”
He quizzes past her towards the radio and commands it to turn itself on and boasts. He continues this door will open by my command of my voice. Listen to this “open door please.” The computer recognises it and the door opens. Are you ready for this he continues to boast and

give the computer all kinds of instruction things you would not believe it could turn your TV on and have the things in the kitchen make your food, lighting on or off with dimmers if need be. Alarm systems and video footage covering every angle this home is as tight as as a bank safe.
"do you want to see more I'll take you down stairs."
"Computer open the stairs." Benjamin request it.
Lucy says tells him to wait and that she has got the picture.
Benjamin says "what."
The girl tells him that she was going to the toilet, as she is in the bathroom. Benjamin is getting cosy and find s some music to play. He tells his system to play the music channel.
Benjamin sits down the girl returns from the toilet all was well for the moment she sits down next to Benjamin, he has a beer she wants a glass of wine. So, who built this house.
"I'm not sure I think I did around three hundred years ago back then all the technology was top stuff the houses of the future I do not know it was probably NASA, they do not exist now it all the company. I have not been here before. She continues
"How do you know your way around the place so well."
"I do not know either I suppose you could intuition." He continues
"It is the address that I was given in fact that is alien the computer brought us here so he probably has the true answer."
She claps her hands and says" lights off". She had not figured it out.
I told her again. "its voice activated"
"Oh yes I forgot."
"He reminds s her again this house is controlled by his voice and his voice alone."
"And the computer." The girl asks
He replies the same.

After the Lucy had taken a good look around feeling impressed the perks of the job I guess then Benjamin shouts alarms systems up the computer compiles.
The computer replies with. "we are now secure."
Benjamin now says that they could relax.
In the morning, he wakes up the girl was still asleep he try's his radio connection but there's still nobody answering. Benjamin is beginning

to worry after an hour or so he tries again again nothing more and more thought of uncertainly enter his head. He is unsure wryer the thoughts wryer coming from the s being told to kill the girl or he was being told that the girl was going to kill him. He disregards the thought but there were many questions that are to himself why he had received the message he was still and relaxed he could handle the pressure. The girl wakes up with Benjamin standing in the room by the window. He begins.

"you were talking in your sleep."

She replies, "I was."

"Yeah you said some really interesting stuff."

"I did not think that I could be so loud it was probably the wine."

"it was something about a river you had to be there."

"was that it." she said

Benjamin replies "yes that was it."

Benjamin ws making it up.

"So, what happens now do you kill me."

Benjamin changes the subject she changes it back she asks him again Benjamin does not answer.

"Can you hand me my dress." She asks him politely.

"I will meet you in the kitchen do you need a coffee."

"No."

He takes a seat in the kitchen and waits for her to join him. She walks in and goes to the fridge taking out a carton. Then speaks.

"Do you have any food."

Benjamin replies. "It's all there in the kitchen help your self-kitchen on." he shouts as he leaves her to cook her breakfast herself.

She seems happy and thanks Benjamin he returns the compliment with silence they were both dreaming of each other but they were both awoken by a large smashing sound.

"There her were back in business."

It was the company they had found us again she shouts out at him as he shouts at her.

"Were safe they cannot penetrate the house it basically a war bunker I forgot to tell you that part."

Lucy was still worried.

Benjamin shouts "weapons up all systems shields."

He ws not to late he trying to calm the girl down so he can hear them and his trying to close his eyes but he needs quiet to visualize what's out there but the girl is still panicking.
He had to shout at her hard to stop her from shouting as he is waiting for her to calm down he walks casually to the computer which is attached to his main systems he still cannot see and he asks the computer for something visual the computer gives him something completely different then he receives the everything at once it was like a system over load to the mind. Benjamin can see there's two on the roof and those fucking aliens are on my front door, there being back up by their space machine and they have weapons big weapons all Benjamin's security was up it was just a matter of time, before Benjamin gets brought in or somebody dies. Benjamin goes to his gun cabinet using the computer to open it. the is still in the kitchen flipping out. He shouts to the girl that they had got company her reply to that was I need the toilet Benjamin smiles he shouts to as the house is being bombarded. The computer tells Benjamin that their shields are down by twenty per centre shouts to her if she was ready to handle a weapon she cries out no his replied to that was now is the time to learn. The space ship above them sounded like close and was getting closer it was it was going to crash in to the house. Benjamin is still at the gun cabinet loading up the array of weapons with amination. He throws as couple of heavy space weapons at the girl with a cocky remark.
"So, you finally decided to turn up."
The girl catches the third gun. They wryer both ready to action. The space ship sounds close, too close for Benjamin to like he knows that they are in trouble. Juta as he grabs the girl and pushes her to the floor a missile hits the building. Benjamin yells to his computer system to put up the homes shields, with all the damage that the first missile had done the computer is damaged and has started to malfunction he shouts again he shouts out to it again.
"get my shields up."
Just as a second missile hits the building blowing Benjamin off his feet. As Benjamin is thrown across the room somehow lands on his feet. He stands in astonishment, he calls out to the computer system again this time he calls shields the computer still damaged manages to receive the order and the shield s come on. The girl is still drunk and is in the kitchen acting crazy. She is pacing up and down frantically repeating in a kind of chant.

"we all going to die."
Benjamin grabs her by her arm and tries to calm her down. She pushes Benjamin off her and continues.
"we have to get out of here. It is your fault all I was doing was trying to walk my dog in which you forced me to disown in the park." She continues. It was your fault my poor, poor doggy."
Benjamin does not know what to say and in terms of calming her down he was pretty shit at it

CHAPTER FOUR

As she finally becomes tired and still in shock sits down. The pirates above realize that their weapons can no longer work on the building. As soon as Benjamin realizes this he sits down and closes his eyes tired after the battle but not out of danger he knows that falling asleep now would be dangerous. The girl Lucy now had already fallen asleep. He nudges her to see if she is asleep then sees that she had been hit by a piece of shrapnel, she must of past out through the pain.
Benjamin was no doctor but he can see that she needed a real medical attention. He calls out to his computer.
"Computer where is my medical kit."
The computer replies.
"it is the kitchen."
Benjamin goes to the kitchen it had been blown apart, Benjamin struggles to find another answer.
He takes her jacket off her and tears it into three pieces then ties up the wound. The girl was in a mess and when she awakes he knows she is not going to be happy. Benjamin tries to wake her and is slowly winning she was slowly coming around she pulls the make shift bandages off Benjamin puts them on again she had no ideas where she was or what was happening. He hands s her a glass of water she pushes a side. Benjamin reties the wound and give s her a glass of water and tries too wake her. He checks her breathing and looks at her eyes her eyes seem to be okay she was now dreaming Benjamin knew this as he was watching her eyes twitching around in her eye lids.

As she begins to awake she rolls over on to her side not knowing but she was forcing herself in to more pain. Benjamin has some paracetamol ready as he knew that she would wake up in pain two

minutes later exactly Lucy wakes up. I knew straight away what she was going to ask for.
Benjamin gives her the glass of water first it was cold and the glass was clear she take the glass clenching it tightly so tight that the glass breaking s in her hand her mouth was shaking as she puts her hand out for the pain killers. Her mouth was shaking as she holds out her hand Benjamin offers her a way out of all the pain she puts the white pills in her mouth, closing her eyes believing that the pain will slowly leave. As she looks around the room that she is in everything is a blur she rubs her head in a dream state her soft hands touching her soft hair it was as if ache was going to come on. Benjamin speaks to her as he is trying to wake her, just to see if she was okay. Then she wakes
"No, no I I'm bloody not okay, where am I." she shouts.
"Great you do not know where you are you do not remember."
"Remember what." She says as she awakes.
"look" Benjamin says, "look at me."
"I cannot explain now okay but you are safe I just hope that your memories come back. Because I have no way of explaining why you are here but you are."
Benjamin looks at the girl the girl Lucy looks at Benjamin, both in silence and both refusing to speak.
"I hope that your memories come back."
Benjamin could feel a breeze the girl could see but said nothing.
"what."
She tries to point at what Benjamin had just felt, Benjamin not knowing that there was somebody behind him. Then he hears him.
"ask her again."
"what". He shouts at her, then catches on Benjamin is marked there was a man at his window he had no weaponeer and there was a man in his garden., which was behind him.
And realizes that the shields in the house had malfunctioned he shouts shields up but instead of a reply from the computer he gets an array of bullets from the mean outside in his garden.
"Benjamin shouts out. " those windows where designer.
The houses windows and designer doors are blown apart. The blast of the gun fire was so advanced it ripped out the whole living area. First the furniture goes then the fire place it continues, there's fire everywhere then the celling then with that falling down Benjamin yells.
"fire."

The sprinklers come on this time the computer understands all the fire exits are opened.
The fire extinguishers then come on. There is water rushing out of the celling, Benjamin picks up the girl and walks out.
The computer then announces
"all systems are working malfunction, malfunction."
All the rooms where filling with water and smoke as he leaves through the last door Benjamin calls out again to the computer.
"All systems close, lock all doors."
The computer complies. As he carries the girl to the car she is biting and hitting him on his back. He then calls out to the computer.
"lock home."
The girl is contempt on hitting Benjamin and telling him to put her down eventually he drops her on to the car park floor by his car. He speaks to his computer and tells it to open the car doors both. the car doors open. The picks herself off the floor and gets in. Benjamin waits for a moment, he looks back at what had happened he gets into the car flicking up his gear stick and pressing the button on it and watches his whole house explode

The shattering explosion awakes the girl.
"your back" he says
"what happened." She asks.
"oh, this and that nothing that I could not handle you know just blowing up my house. It's an everyday thing nothing to worry about."
She leans back and then across Benjamin and gives him a kiss on the cheek, Benjamin smiles and thanks her.
"I'm back." She continues with the compliment.
They drive out of the drive watching the house burn, the girl Lucy lays down still she is bleeding Benjamin asks her if she is alright.

"no." she says. "no, I'm not I'm still bleeding. What have you done." She shouts.
"take me a hospital need stitching up."
Benjamin puts his foot down as they speed through the traffic Lucy tells Benjamin to hurry up as she believes that she is in danger of losing her life as she passes out for the second time. As she awakes Benjamin is no closer Benjamin sus jest that he should do the operation her reply to that was are you out of your mind.
"I can pull over we are not going to make it let me do the operation."
Benjamin pulls the car over he repeats seriously "where is your medical pack."
She replies
"In the fucking glove compartment. I can operate myself."
Benjamin looks inside the glove compartment it is all there, a load of medical stuff. The girl gets out of the car Benjamin stays put as he watches her going into shock. As she come s around the car and gets into the back seat.
"you can drive now." She says.
Benjamin adjusts the rear-view mirror not taking his eyes off the girl and watching her
Cutting herself open and applying to the wound. Again, Benjamin pulls over the girl get out of the passage seat into the front passage seat and tells Benjamin to drive she insists.
"where are we going."
"I do not know yet. I have a friend up in the wood she might be able to tell me what the chip is and why the pirates want me and you dead. They killed that guy in the park in cold blood it was obvious to me that the chip is of some important, he might be able to tell me what's on it I am now going to sleep the car is on auto pilot so sit back and relax do not touch anything."
"pull up ill drive it will keep me from the pain."
"what."
"I said pull up ill drive. I have had enough of computers for one night voice activated systems.
"Okay."
Benjamin pulls his verse over and they swap seats, Benjamin falls asleep almost straight away. the girl looks down on the dash board and speaks to herself as Benjamin falls father in to the dream he had passed out completely due to all then action the girl Lucy continues knowing that Benjamin is out for the count.

“right where are we.” She is acting unprofessional. She continues with the computer.
“are there any lodges up in the mountains.” Knowing that she had found her desi station she puts her foot down. As she drives she keeps her eyes on Benjamin. Benjamin is dreaming of the future. He was dreaming of the girl and her future also this was the only way to protect the girl, and the microchip.
“what could I see, reflections of the mind voices through the mind I had to tell myself every day I have a mind please do not abuse it.” Benjamin was talking in his sleep.
“that is an interesting conversation that you are having.”
Benjamin awakes with a jump something scared him Lucy realizes that Benjamin is in trouble the girl continues.
“hay calm down your safe. You are home now.”
He wakes up slowly drooling out the side of his mouth and continues with.
“was I dre4aming dis I speak or should I say was I talking.”
“a little here and there.” She said.
Benjamin reply’s “take no notice it is usual for me it come s with the job. I’m not in to making excuses I should just say I am a sleep talker I’ve been doing it since I was a kid.”
“What did you dream.”
“that’s none of your business, I mint that’s a little personal. And it’s none of your concern.”
“come on I saw you twitching.”
“with everything that has happened you would think that I possibly might have just a few worries. Any way like I said its none of your concern.”

As Benjamin slowly awakes the girl gets out of the car Benjamin stays in the car the girl then walks confidently toward s the house Benjamin is content on staying out, he does not move. Benjamin is in fear he knows that something is wrong. He closes his eyes and with a second

he sees it. the house is rigged with explosives the girl is happy that they had escaped as she believes that they had escaped. Benjamin must move quickly as he retakes control of his mind he too gets out of the car the space virile as she makes her way to the front door Benjamin shouts, telling her.
“do not move.” He calls out not knowing if she heard him he calls again. She does not listen and continues toward the front door. As she continues toward the door he shouts out again do not move. Then she realities that something was wrong she pauses and asks him, she guessed it already and froze to a standstill.
“Do not move, an inch.” Benjamin shouts.
“I’m coming to get you be calm and stay still.”
They both then realises that the place is rigged and ready to blow. With all the pressure, the girl bows down and take a step backwards Benjamin yells.
“do not move I will come and get you.”
Lucy cannot take the pressure or the frith=gut of being still and not moving she tries with all her strength but she is still too frightened to keep still. Before Benjamin can get to her she takes s exactly two more steps not backward as you would expect but forwards her movements as Benjamin presumed set of the explosives just as Benjamin was just about to grab her. The explosion is a small one and Benjamin again take s it as a warming as they both hit the deck, Benjamin is on fire and must put himself out while the girl Lucy had a slight case of shell shock. Both patting each other down and escaping injury. There were pieces of wood and dare everywhere Benjamin believes that they were being set up.
Benjamin shouts out the girl is hurt all over again, Benjamin picks her up again half-conscious she speaks out.
“I hate you Benjamin.” The girl passes out. Benjamin continues.
“Well I hate you too but you have to really start listening as your problem will be the death of the both of us. Now can you walk as the pirates as you call them will be on our tail within a minute.”
Benjamin pushes her hair aside and picks her up struggling to put her back of the space verse.
“give me the microchip.”
The girl gives s him the microchip but not straight away as it is lodged in her bra.
“do you have it.”
“Yes, I do, here.”

CHAPTER FIVE

Benjamin watches the house as it burns, the smoke hitting the wind screen with the flames as it slowly burned as the flames slowly subsisted he looks at his gear stick for no reason while putting the gears into reverse then turns on
his window wipers to wipe the soot from the explosion off his wind screen. Benjamin sits there and the girl that I wanted to heal me had passed out again. Benjamin looks inside of the glove compartment it is all in to his mind as he looks over his shoulder at the girl Lucy the girl seems to be able to get away with death as she is injured again. On the other hand, his arm had been damaged, he looks in the compartment of the dash board one handed as he snuffles through what was left of what was then bandages that he used before for the girl stitched herself up with. There was not much left over. Then it dawns upon him why was there medical equipment about him, he not to embarrassed to question it, he continues to think it was like he was a big coincidence everything fitted Benjamin was thinking that it was too smooth too normal, there was something wrong. something did not feel right., and it had something to do with the girl.
he touched the bandages and closes his eyes in an instant he sees the image. Benjamin sees that he has nothing for the moment he beliefs now that he is being set up. He s tries his intercom to his headquarters but gets nothing. There's no answer Benjamin continues to worry. The girl is still half conscious in the passage side of his car, Benjamin was slowly dropping off to sleep also. Benjamin finds the right state of mind to reverse out of the drive way backwards as he looks at the blown-up mess that was in front of him. There was another explosion as he turns the car out of the long drive the house was destroyed. Benjamin drives down his drive as he nears the gate of what was his home he tells his computer to open the gates. He has no idea where is is going or what his destination is.
"computer." Benjamin says.
"yes Benjamin." It replies
"Are there any hotels in the area."
The computer malfunctions the computer switches off, Benjamin does not know yet that the microchip has a homing device built in to it.

which explains how and why they keep on being found every time they escape. He puts the car on automatic drive and studies the microchip as they head for their new destination. He closes his eyes and parses the chip looking for answers. It takes s him to a new world the things that he sees are incredible things that he cannot explain. As he leaves the vision which is of the future, he meets the girl. The girl that he has beside himself. He enters her mind and finds even more. She is not the innocent girl in the park that he thinks or thought. As Benjamin continues through her mind not forgetting the images of the worlds future and knowing that he was breaching her privacy. He opens his eyes and comes straight back, the girl flops straight upon him he gentry pushes her off in to a better position in the car seat. Benjamin is board of driving within a few seconds he has his car back to auto pilot again he feels tired and he wants to sleep. He knows that he is a target with the girl. He places the microchip down onto his dashboard. Making sure that keeping the microchip at a distant so it would not be contaminated threw human touch. Benjamin closes his eyes as he sleeps he dreams of the girl that is beside him. As he dreams of the stars which are before him an are above him. Not knowing how to answer them. there is a reason that he is there but he cannot understand them. the dream changes he is falling back to the planet back into the past he begins to think of his past he dreams of his family with his children and wife.

After the death of his wife he was tired and sent into deep freeze, he already knew that he had been set up. And it looks like it was all happening again. The judge and jury did not understand his side of the story there was a verdict life imp resentment in a deep freeze. He knew that he was being set up again. The people that killed his family and framed him were still out there. There was an image stuck in him but it was a blur. He could not make any sense as he could not see it the vision clearly but deep down inside he knew. As the more he tries to visualise the less the image became. At that moment Benjamin wakes wiping the tears from his face. he is sitting in his car gripping the steering wheel. He looks over his shoulder the girl is still out. He takes off his driving gloves Lucy looks like she is asleep. He wipes s the tears which are still running down his face again. Benjamin is clearly upset, but is happy that the girl is asleep and did not know. Benjamin looks outside the car window and focuses it had begun to rain, he checks with his computer his where about the computer tells him.

Benjamin is not through crying as each tear runs down his face, it was like each memory that he has ever had. He was clearly getting upset. He continues to check with the computer there ware about.
To his astonishment the computer had taking them both to his father's house. He knew straight away and asks his computer.
"Computer why are we here."
The computer answers. "It was the only safe place that my system has for you and it was the nearest. I took it that you did not have an acquired destination so I brought here. So, I took the liberty of calling your dad. Hence that's why you are here. I knew that you would be pleased."
The computer turns its self-off. Benjamin is greeted by his father.
"hay son how is you."
"hello father I'm sorry that bloody computer if you know what I mean."
Before Benjamin can but in his father, has welcomed them into his home. his father continues,
"You do not have to worry the computer has told me everything."
"it did."
"yeah it did now get the girl inside and I will attend to her wounds. Oh, and cover the car as there can be some strange people around here. I do not like alien beings. And I do not want them around here."
Benjamin does as he is told he picks up the large plastic sheeting and calls out to his dad.
"it would be easier if we just shoved it in the garage."
His father replies that it is occupied.

Benjamin did not take the con=vernation any further, it's raining still and windy he struggles and just manages to cover the car. Leaving a few bricks to hold down the sheets.
The night was extremely dark, darker than usual it was like an eclipse. It looked like it was going to be a thunder storm. Benjamin pulls his hood up over his head as he heads upstairs to his father's door, off the balcony it was reminding Benjamin of when he was a child sitting in his father's rocking chair and playing music. As he climbed each step each step had a reminded him of his childhood. As he makes it to the top he pulls his hood down.
"there's a storm brewing, and I think its heading our way."

There is a pause, then his father speaks.
“the girl does not look to okay, what happened to her.”
“oh, not to mush a celling fell on top of her and a couple of bullets she is stronger she tried to stitch herself up on the motor way side she insisted and would not let me touch her.”
“she is hardly breathing.”
“Does she need a doctor.”
“I do not know.”
Benjamin take is a good look at her.
“Where did she come from she is not your girlfriend.”
“I found her in the park.”
“Back to back told me to follow her until I received this chip.”
“what chip.”
Benjamin does not answer; the girl is on the sofa she is not looking any better but looked like she would pull through.
“Come on, come through to the living room.”

Benjamin has already sensed something but he continues to follow his dad to the living room. As Benjamin keeps his distant. His farther continues.
“So where did you find her.”
Benjamin replies that he had already answered that question. Then he continues.
“it is a long story dad.”
They continue with talking into the night towards the early hours of the morning. Benjamin is already questioning his farther. He knew that something had changed as Benjamin’s real father was not a drinker and the man in front of him had been knocking them back. He also knew as the man on front of was wearing a san Francisco American forty miners cap except his real father was a LA raiders fan. He continues knowing that there was something wrong Benjamin’s real farther was into horses yet when Benjamin looked outside there were no horses. As he looked outside from a window the paddock=k was not there. The paddock that he grew up with. Benjamin insists that he should go down to the cellar for some more drink a bottle or a co0uple of bottle of wine. Also, his farther had asked to many questions to be his father. Benjamin says to himself as he walks toward the caller doors that the man in front of him was not his father. As he went to the cellar door the man in front of him changed the subject I had to ask him what was he hiding. That was not my father’s way. His symptoms

began to set in whatever it was it was just about to malfunction, I knew at that point as all the speaking fast and all its questions now made sense. And was all part of the process, it would not stop speaking, and it would not stand still. As it neared to the end of its malfunction, its word s became harder to listen too.
It was clear to me now that it was droid a robot. As I asked it not telling it yet that I knew what it was. I refused to move from the cellar door and it seemed to make it angry. I knew that there was something up. Then it happened it was walking towards me at a great speed shouting get out of the way. I stood firm not shifting an inch and questioned its actions, I looked straight into its eyes, I knew then that this was not my father in all the commotion I raised my hands, I had to make the first move.
There was some fungi Fu as I went to hit him three-time s s in one move, it lent back forcing me to switch sides with it he was now facing the door as he went for the door. The fight went to the kitchen where he knew what I was doing he reached for a set of knifes which he intende3d to use before the fight had even started. He pulls out the biggest knife that I had ever seen.
"shit" I said. "Come on." I said.
He took a swipe at me he missed as I lent backwards then he took another just missing me. as I moved back father I was at the door again but I had my back to it. he was quick as quick as me I was wondering if I had found my match. I then knocked one of the knifes out of his hand, but there was more that happened with my foot. As I was stepping back quickly then suddenly moving forward, and doing it all over again I finally disarmed him. As it launched another attack he was now doing the punching and I was on the defiance. This was happening to me two then three times each punch e=weakening me. he had not reached my body yet everything that he had given me to take was in the face or there about. We moved in synchronism each block and each kick and pouch. I was reasonably tired and needed the girl as it happens she was woken through the noise of things smashing such as plates and glass windows and kitchen wear. The girl Lucy was shouting and came to find me, she had a big shock. The robot had locked the door she had found me but had no way of getting to me. although I could hear her shouting,
"Benjamin are you there."
I replied to her" yes I am in here but I'm a little busy now."
"Are you there I did not hear you are you okay." She calls out.

As she forces the door bumping Benjamin back into fighting position. As he hits the robot as hard as he can and still managing to stay on his feet. The girl walks in with a piece of wood.
“where did you get that from.” Benjamin asks.
“from the fire place.” Lucy says.
The robot grabs Benjamin from behind throwing him through the wall of the kitchen as he hits the deck and the robot is going after him he shouts out. She hits the robot hard on its back it falls to rhea ground Benjamin is just picking himself up ache grabs the girl in time. Benjamin was ready for one more round the girl insists that they should go. But that was not it.
“Come on let’s get out of here “the girl shouts.
Benjamin decides to wait he tells the girl hat there’s is something wrong. he tells her again that he feels it. Benjamin rolls over the droid as he looks at it infect staring at it, he speaks to it, the girl intervenes.
“What is it.”
The girl interrupts,
“what.”
Benjamin rolls the droid over and tries to look at it he insists that the girl turns around as he open the robot droids head, as he sticks his hand into his brain he says quietly that this is not my father. He insists that Lucy should turn away again as she is peaking. Lucy turns around, Benjamin implies that she might not like what she is going to see. Lucy turns around.
Benjamin tells her that he is looking for his chip he was looking for another microchip he did not find one it did not make sense. He pulls his hand out of his head. As they were getting ready to leave as the home a=was un safe Benjamin hear a sound he tells the girl to turn around she turns around and asks her.
“Did you hear that.”
“What.”
“That sound.”
Benjamin turns to the cellar doors.
“Wait I can hear something.”
“You’re not going down there.”
“There is something down there I have to look.”
“Suits me.”
“Hay chill, I think I’ve just found my father.”
Benjamin starts tapping on the walls everyone eventually the girl hers it too. Benjamin know is that there was someone down there in his

cellar it sounded like it was human he calls out his father name and continues to approach the cellar. The cellar is locked so Benjamin must pick the lock. Eventually he opens the door and with a lot of luck finds his father he finds his dad. As he calls out his father's name they are reunited. Benjamin and his father and girl leave the cellar he is overwhelmed with the presents of his son. He gives s Benjamin a big hug with thanks. Benjamin take ships father upstairs to discuss what had happened and decide s weather or not it was safe for his father to stay in his home his dad says and tells Benjamin that he would have no other place to go. The girl butts in saying that his father could ride with them.

"may be its safe now to stay here now."
"it is an option do you feel safe."
"Yes, but a dangerous one." The girls said.
"do me a favour go check if the car is still there I'm going to make a phone call."
"Who me." Benjamin father says confused.
"no not you the girl."
The girl was wounded but she had the bottle to walk to the car, she shouts out, "it's all there Benjamin."
Benjamin shouts back "is it all there."
She replies "yes, it is it's all there."
Lucy walks back from the car and into the house nothing but this time Benjamin a=has a wound. The girl Lucy oils Benjamin aside away from his dad.
"look." She says.
Benjamin is hesitant, she continues,
"Look at me." she insists and continues. "I am not in the business of being shit up I can put up with all the cation that you like but walking into the dark towards a car that could explode it's just not me do you understand me."
With that the girl slaps Benjamin around the face Benjamin is in shell shock through all the excitement and cannot speak. And does nothing as his father smiles and says nothing. Then he says stupidly.
"I do not know maybe you two would make a nice couple."
Benjamin continues.
"Look dad something is wrong with the company that they had to freeze me to council the truth they had me waiting on this girl Lucy. They had me watching her that's why I am back. That is the only

reason that I am here. But everywhere we go there is destruction and murder. All I have is this microchip can you make anything of it. Because every time I unload my mind I'm in the same position I am left with the same thing it reloads with the dead guys and destruction." My boss at back to back are ignoring me, they will not answer my calls and when they do something bad always happens. I finally realized that there as nobody was on the other end.
My father said to me to be brave and it and everything will be okay, it was alright and we were in a safe place. He cony=tined where are those idiots they will out come back again. He continued I'm going to stick it outside .it will be like guy folks and I'll watch the money coming in as this bastard burn. Benjamin gives his father a hug and explains that he must go he apologises. As his father sets up a bomb fire to burn the android copse wishes him lick and tells him to be safe. Benjamin give s smile and another hug just to make sure. his father says his good bye as the Lucy is trying to say her there's kind of a Hussle with hugging and good byes. The girl walks out not knowing what to think and is still bleeding. Benjamin uncovers his car and tells the girl Lucy to get in. as he throws the tarpaulin a side. The has something to say.
"I really think that we should stay at your dads it seems to be a good place to stay and I like him he is cool."
"I'm not putting my family in danger if they are following us then its going to be on their ground not my fathers, you said that if you knew something."

CHAPTER SIX

"Where are we going."
"We are heading up into the mountains. I have one safer house there nobody knows about it we should be safe there. The only way of getting to once they are there is by rope."
"in that case how will we get there."
"By rope as it is up a mountain."
"Yeah of course." The girl thinks he's joking. When she finds out that he is serious "your joking right."
"No wrong."

Before they leave the house in the forest Benjamin's dad tells him that there is a tone of rope in the garage Benjamin t6ells him that he

already knows and has told the girl Lucy the plan. His dad continues you into the mountains Benjamin already knew this. Benjamin knows that he cannot hind forever and is agreeing to his plan before he leave he makes a store to his father by touching his head with his head joking. And just says.
"just checking."
His dad smiles and they give each other their good byes. Benjamin gets into his car.
"As I understand that the verses that they are using according to these plans and images their verses can only hover to approximately three hundred feet,

"and."
"well the according to this map we are approximately twenty thousand feet. we will need some rope."
"Are you sure." The girl reply's.
"Pretty much so." The computer reply's.
"it's a long way up there but I think we can do it." The cars hovering by the side of the mountain the girls grabbing the ropes from the back of the car.
"How it did you know we wryer going to end up here Benjamin."
"Benjamin."
Benjamin answers "I did not know."
Benjamin leave the car on hover mode and cleverly removes the computer from the dash board. As he stuffs it in to his jacket. They start climbing, after an hour the girl has something to say.
"did you think that we could have started the climb in the morning." Lucy shouts.
"no, I did not think that we would have that much time." Benjamin replies
"come do really think that they would follow us up here." Lucy
"Anything is possible." Benjamin.

"I have the feeling that they can find us anywhere as every time we escape they seem to find us.
They have found us in all of my safe houses. They even found my fathers."

The snow blows down and a wind picks up. Lucy continues.
"it would be nice if we could stop until the morning."
"Are you kidding me Lucy this is brilliant you cannot tell me you are not enjoying the adrenaline."
Lucy and Benjamin keep on climbing. As they come together Benjamin hands her something.
"here take this."
"What is it."
"It is a heat pack, it will keep you warm. You activate it by pushing it down beachful as it only lasts an hour or two."
As the Lucy plays around with she drops the heat pack.
"shit, dam," Lucy shouts and continues. "I've lost it."
"Lost what." Benjamin shouts.
"I've lost the heat pack." Lucy shouts.
"Okay do not worry you can have mine." she gives him a minute to catch up. Just as they finish the conversation the heat pack just hits Benjamin shoulder he thinks it was snow but catches it anyway. When he looks at it he finds that it was the her heat pack.
He calls to Lucy. "hay guess what."
"what" was her reply.
"I have something for you. I have something for you I have saved your heat pack."
The girl continues to ad sale down too him. She retrieves the heat pack. Benjamin and Lucy are now climbing side to side again for another hour. He was thinking that she was good and even for the injury he had guts and determination to win. I knew inside she wanted to get to the top of the mountain. They both climb together for a while until the girl gets back into pace. And climbs leaving Benjamin behind. He loses sight of her. But only for a moment as there a change in the weather. There's a small snow storm. He calls out to her but this time there's no answer.
He shouts out loud again realizing that If he shouts out veto loud that he would cause an avalanche.
He tries again and eventually finds and there together again.
"Are you okay." Benjamin asks her.
"Yes I'm fine." She says.
"Please do not do that again you scared the life out of me. if I call you answer me. I thought that I had lost you."

“ Okay I have found a whole in the mountain, so can we rest now. I think we should stay here, I cannot climb any further I’m too tired.” She’s plods with Benjamin until he agrees.
Benjamin pauses and gives himself time to think and waits for answer.
“I think we should climb it cannot be that far now to the top but while we are here we can take a break.”
The girl disagrees and they discuss it further until Benjamin bows down.
“Okay do you think that we can make the tent in here.” Benjamin says.
“Yes I do.” She smiles.
The girl has found a cave of ice and the floor is sturdy to stamp on. They agree to set up the tent. The girl of on one again.
“Good you understand me.” she continues.
The computer has some information for Benjamin, the message was that they were being followed but the computer had frozen with the cold and Benjamin does not get the message for some time.
The girl had put the tent up and now was onto Benjamin about building a fire. Benjamin answers her.
“was that a stupid question.” Replies Benjamin.
“Yes I meant to say let’s cuddle up and get warm.” The changes her herb.”
“Yes well I was just about to say we have enough heat packets to last us until the morning.”
The girl Lucy does not answer they struggle up to each other Benjamin tells her that they will leave early in the morning the girl wants to close her eyes but is worried as the night time temperature drops. Benjamin agrees it is a little too cold just to close your eyes it will only be a couple of hours before the morning arises. Then they could climb again.

The sun arises and the moon and the darkness disappears behind the sun. the power of the light with the reflection of snow his Benjamin’s mind. They both attar climbing again. The snow is wet, icy and slippery. But they were both determined to reach the top. The girl was moving fast leaving Benjamin behind her he calls out.
“hay this is not a race, can you slow down.” To Benjamin’s surprise she calls back to him.
“it is just as spring as any other sport.”
“Who said anything about sports.” Benjamin smiles. And continues up the mountain.

The girl continues the conversation.
"What the matter are you struggling to keep up."
"That sounded like a challenge." Benjamin says shouting loudly, forgetting that where he was.
Eventually Benjamin catches up with the girl both back to back.
"are you okay." The girl says.
"yes I'm fine just a little cold."
"how far to the top."
"I'm sure by the shape of that rock about a mile." Benjamin shivers.
The answers with excitement. " are you serious."
"Pretty much so yes." Benjamin answers her.
They both keep on climbing as the elements begin to take control of the climb. Fighting the mountains as its starts to snow again. For some strange reason Benjamin feel danger again he thinks that something is wrong he could not reach his computer as it was too cold. It would be able to tell him what was wrong but his mind already knew. They are now by each other side s.
He calls to the girl.
"Look stay close I think that there is something wrong."
"What is it."
"I do not know exactly but I can feel danger."
"Is another avalanche."
"No this is a totally different feeling."
Suddenly from know where a huge gust of wind hammers the mountain and Benjamin is blown off the face. as he goes he grabs the girl, who in return garbs him saving from the blast of the wind.
"Just in time, I thought you were gone. Are you okay. "
"Just a little shaken. I knew that hit was going to happen I just had a feeling."
As they continue to climb the wind settle down again and the sky's clear and the sun comes out. But not for long.
This time the wind got too strong for her also as within a few second the wind picked up again as the sun went in and darkness fell upon them again a large gust of wind blows her of the mountain as she falls down Benjamin feels her rip past him with her rope, Benjamin braces his self for second as he knows that if he did not get his pick in they would both go. Benjamin calls out to her. She seems okay she catches up with him. They start talking blaming each other then decide that it was the wind rather than Benjamin.

“I hope this is worth it as I am now stick of climbing when can we rest.” She says.
“Do not worry, I can see the top.”
“You obviously have great eyes because that is not the top.”
“Yes it is.”
“No its not.”
“Yes it is be quiet we are nearly there.”
The girl Lucy shuts up and keeps on climbing, as Benjamin nears the top. He reaches down into his jacket one handed, his hands cold and shaking with the cold of the extreme weather, even with his gloves on. He turns the computer on.
“The computer speaks “it good to be back how have you been.”
“Yes, it nice to hear you.”
“what is going on up there.”
The computer scans the area, it tells Benjamin that the area is clear and safe the computer tells Benjamin that there is a lodge up there and there are no civilians there. As he pulls himself on to the soft edge the girl follows him the girl was happy that they had reached the top although she was still in pain.
“yes, we have made it” the slays to Benjamin.
“Pretty much so come on let’s get inside leave the rope for later.” Benjamin walks toward the
Building. Benjamin is first to the lodge as he uses his computer to check it all out making it safe for the girl. He has a nose a sentinel nose. He makes his way down stairs in the lodge to the cellar. He finds an electrical box, he plays around with it for a minute until he finds the right switch and gives the lodge power, he then returns upstairs and continues as he turns on the lights. As he makes the cheeks he tells the Lucy to put build a fire.
“We should be safe here everything is in order.” Benjamin tells her. The girl Lucy answers him” yes but for how long it so obvious that we are being followed. How long before the bad guys finally catch up with us. Do you think that I am stupid? How are we going to defend ourselves?”

Benjamin is astonished a says nothing as he in is his element and finally feeling relaxed and warm again. He says to her.
“Look we are over a thousand feet up way up on top off to a mountain I’m sure that I would see them coming I’m not saying that they are not

coming as they are properly are this place just give s me and you enough time to think where we will go next."
"that's not an excuse are we really safe because I do not feel it."
"okay we are safe I have had my computer check out everything, I have connected him or it to everything electronical within the next twenty-mile s and at this moment there nothing but snow. We have enough fuel to last a month and there's plenty of food now would you believe me that we are safe."
The girl is finally believing Benjamin and is pleased, Benjamin looks at her wound it was still bleeding. He helps her to red dress the wound. He asks her if she was okay he tells her that he knows that she had taken a few bullets she replies that they wryer just scrapes. Then insist s that she is okay and tells him that his apologies are a bit late.
"I'm fine."
Benjamin goes to the living area the girl wants to take a shower. So, she did Benjamin is surrounded by white sheets everything was cover =end to protect it as he removes the covers from everything this was on going throughout the house except for the fire place. As he removes s the sheets unveiling a ton of ethnology TVs and sound systems, his dad must have been into some seriously loud listening. As he continues in to the kitchen he unravels more. There was a massive gun collection built in tot one of the walls. Benjamin asks the computer to find the codes so that he can unlock it.
He could see clearly what he was looking at, Automatic, Uzi, barrette, shotguns there was even a missile launcher which brought the odd memory back.

CHAPTER SEVEN

He was just about to speak when the girl walked in half dressed in a towel around her.
"This is not good. Guns normally mean trouble." Benjamin is speechless for the first time."
"I think we should leave as soon as possible". He states.
"I do not believe it we have only just got here." there's a pause from both then she answers. I do not know maybe your right." She continues we are better up here than down there who ever had this place set was obvious scared of something and certainly mint to do business."

"Yes, it was my dad's place."
A few weeks later.
The girl was healing up nicely the girl did not let it bother it even though he continued to tell that she looked fine according to her wounds.
"It still hurts though." the finally answers, Benjamin stays quiet as he doe s not what to say. Then he implies that the girl was looking for some sympathy he does express what was in his next thought. But insist that he should give him answer. So, he does.
"I'm sure that you will be okay." he says in a half caring way.
It made Lucy feel better Benjamin realizes that she needs comforting and slips down the sofa next to her. And puts his arm around her shoulder he continues.
"You do not have to worry it is going to be oaky."
"Look no tears okay I do not do tears."
"It's not that, I'm just fed up of being on the run I was fine in then park and all of this running its just wearing me out do you see do you understand me I just want my dog back and to go home. I am fed up of being blown up, I'm hurt and that stupid microchip thing, I cannot take it anymore."
The girl Lucy end s up in tears.
"I just want you to take me home."
She continues for an hour totally breaking down and in Benjamin's arms.

Benjamin falls asleep soon after her it was not unusual for Benjamin to dream the bad guys the pirates were coming and were still figuring out how to get to the top of the mountain as there save machines could not fly that high. Benjamin boss is the only other person that knows were Benjamin is. Benjamin has yet to learn that not only does he have the microchip from the dead guy in the park he has one planted in him he does not know this and that's why he cannot explain how he keeps on being found, and cannot hide. And that's the reason why the pirates keep on finding him.

"I want Benjamin dead."
"Then why did you de freeze him."
"I needed him to get the microchip."
"Fail me again and your dead."
"How do we find them."
"I know exactly where he is doing you need an address find him."
"This time we will kill him and I will bring you both the microchips."
"What about the girl."
"Bring her to me, alive."
"Master, what is on the microchip."
"none of your business.do as you are told."
The one that is standing next to the other steps forwards I can do a better job send me their boss stops for a second to think then he agrees.
"you go with him."
"I cannot wait to see the look on Benjamin's face as and when he dies, find them both and bring them to me. you can go but do not fail me."
The bad guys and the pirates leave for the mountain with their new assassin Benjamin and the girl did not know that their time on the mountain was running short. They wryer in danger again.
A few days later the bad guys and the pirates find the bottom of the mountain, Benjamin was right their space machines did not hack=vet the power to get too the top. After a few more days preparing they finally decide to make an ascend. Benjamin's security is on and through his computer can hear everything.
"We have business there here."
"What, here as in here on the doorstep."
"Not exactly how long did it take us to climb up here."
"about two and a half days."
"Then there two and a half days away."
"How do you know can you be for certain."
"I left camera s in the face of the mountain as we made the ascended up, the computer knows everything he very clever and ninety percent of the time he is right." Benjamin explains. That they have little time

left. Benjamin also tells her by his computer that depending on how fast they climb would be how long they had left in the lodge. Even so that they were well prepared. Benjamin and the girl start to celebrate the rest of their time together. As Benjamin and the continue to party as the evening dawns on them they know that they have very little time they cony=tenue knowing that they are in danger. Benjamin is dancing around.

"I did not know you could dance."

"Come on dance with me it might be your last chance."

The girl Lucy decides to decline then Lucy agrees.

"Okay go easy on me." she insists. "I'm still hurt."

They start dancing again, eventually she is relaxed and enjoying herself, they booth fall onto the sofa. Both are drunk. Now everybody expects them to get closer. The girl blows Benjamin out and head for the kitchen for a bottle of wine but cannot find it.

"Where is it." she asks

"Where's what." Benjamin is upset that she blew him out

"The wine she says you know."

"What."

"I would like another drink." She implies

Benjamin wants to question her; the girl is drunk he begins with. How much have you had to drink he asks her not concerned? She answers him

"a bottle or two."

"He asks her again is that one bottle or two bottles"?

"She wakes up well if I'm honest I have had one whole bottle."

Benjamin smiles. But I have not I have had couple of glasses. She replies half handing her facial expression.

"Come on the truth. "Benjamin says.

"that's it okays a bottle and that all."

Known that she had lies=end he walks down tom the caller for another bottle. he ws thinking that if she had kid once she had lied before and if she had stolen then she would properly do it again not that she had stolen anything that Ice had knew about. But that was a good question. Benjamin continues to discuss the theory again as he is down the cellar. As he picks up the bottle of wine as he is drunk any way he climbs up the cellar stairs to be greeted by her.

"Hello." he says as he is greeted. "your wine my dear, enjoy."

“Thank you.” She said and continues come on lets party. Benjamin checks out with his computer just to make sure that they are still safe and the bad guys are way down the mountain.
Her word s was” lets party.”
Benjamin is busy partying, now the girl knows that the bad guys are homing in and within a few hours in all the excitement he passes out, on his computer system. As he is drunk, the girl is fine Benjamin is out cold seriously she pours the rest of the drink down the sink. The girl Lucy had, had enough also. The girl grabs Benjamin and turns him over he looked well enough and she thought that he was reasonable good looking, and as he was asleep wanted to kiss him knowing that she had an excuse which would be I thought you had stopped breathing and I was resuscitating you would be a good one if she got caught. She slowly and carefully lifts Benjamin off the stereo system that his past out on. Dumping him on the sofa she says to him.
“you look a little uncomfortable there”, as she moves him into a more comfortable position. Benjamin is still out cold she’s temped to empty his jacket and as she thought of it again needed an excuse what would this excuse be. I was just cheeking that you were okay. It did not sound right she disregard she thought but only for the moment. She lifts his wallet while grabbing his ass.
Lucky that he was still out cold and now was asleep, she opens his wallet inside was a badge it said CYBER POLICE. It had his name on it it was true he was who he said he was. She slips the wallet back into his jacket but not where he would no=rally keep it. and not in his trousers where it was before she had picked it. she realizes this but does not have time as he is waking up. Lucy tries it anyway but she had to be quick. She rolls him over as he awakes as he groans she slaps his face just so she could reach his pocket. She was being quick. Hoping that the slap in the face would send him back to sleep. Rather than waking him up she makes another attempt to put the wallet back in its original place. As just as she manages to put the wallet back in to the right place he awakes.
“that was some real hard partying we should do that again some time.” Benjamin makes a statement.
“Am I awaking.” He asks her.
“Yes, your awake big boy. Did you enjoy the party?”
“Come on let’s get our stuff and get out of here they will be hearing in a few hours.”
The girl wipes the smile off her face then Benjamin changes his mind.

"infect we have enough gun power do you think that we should stay."
Benjamin's hang over is upon him.
He stands up then he sits down then tells her.
"You know that we have company do you not."
"Company."
"Yeah those bad boys are on their way up here."
"I'm to shit faced to do anything." So, if you do not mind I'll stay put for now. Lucy realities that achoo is not Benjamin's Favourite friend and has to sober him up ,quickly.
Benjamin does not know the time and asks her if it is late he replies that it is the morning he questions it early or late she tells him that it is early. He replies good, they will not be here until the late evening leaving us a good seven hours head start. Agreed,
"Agreed."
"Are we in danger." The girl says
Benjamin does not answer at first then say "close."
"Who is it she asks him. Is it the pirates the bad guys she says."
"The same as usual."
Benjamin replies it IS the pirates.
"Both of them." she says
Benjamin smiles.
"not both of them all of them the computer is picking up a large numerous detection properly about a hundred men all heading our way."
The computer scans the area and notices a new person the party as so does Benjamin. Benjamin speaks to the computer.
As the computer speaks with Benjamin.
"We have a new visitor." They say the same, " they have sent us the assassin."
"Who."
the girl says I have heard of him."
"Who else"
"I do not know but that guy is the first guy in the lines of assassin is who you say he is your dead. He can find you anywhere especially if you meet him."
"Well that's great let's hope that I do not have to meet him. I believe that he has the same mind power as you."
So, who is he
"He is an assassin. properly the best of the best."
"how do you know."

"Look it's been an interesting morning let's get out of here before we are blown apart."
Benjamin believes that he has had a dream and tries to explain to Lucy that he has seen the future. his future she understands and tells him that it was only a dream and it might not happen. In return Benjamin tells that most of the dreams he has normally happen. This scares her and she is taken back. Lucy doe s not know what to say. There is a pause they are both silence. Benjamin resides from gab=vying her the truth he no longer trusts her. As the girl looks up she looks happy. He wants to know what had made her this way he asks her a question.
"Why are you smiling did I say something funny."
"She replies that you are making me laugh."
He continues. "what you think the predictive that we are in is funny."
She continues "it was just a dream okay nothing more nothing less." She says.
Benjamin is trying to explain that the dreams that he had were not dreams but real visions. in the end, the girl walks out after telling Benjamin to turn himself off she was fed up of trying to explain.

CHAPTER EIGHT

He approaches her again in the kitchen as she holds her posture knowing that Benjamin was fighting back, and hanging on to a facial expression which Benjamin buys. Benjamin tries to explain again he continues he insist again that his dreams were real, there is no answer from Lucy. They continue the debate. And it lasts into the evening eternally she agrees and the debate is over. Benjamin knows that she is handing something and does not take the thought any further which by him was a big mistake he does not know yet that she is in the inside.as the evening come s on the second day and as they have decided to hold their ground Benjamin is sober again and the girl wants to keep on partying, she is putting it on. Benjamin stays level headed and insists that partying is only for the weekend. And for now, it is over. He sits down and closes his eyes not knowing what he is going to see. and what he does see blows him away. he can see the girl Lucy with a gun

and she is pointing at him. He opens his eyes keeping the vision to himself as he reaches for his wallet and cannot find it at first, he believes that he has missed placed at first. Then the girl walks in straight away he knew and straight away she knew and he knew that she knew. She knew because she was good and he knew because she was that good. As Benjamin looks upwards he knows that he is in danger he wants to question her but the timing was all wrong the dad gutsy were getting closer and there was not the time for a one to one in pick pocketing. He decides to time his approach even though he finds his wallet in his jacket pocket and not his trousers back pocket where he normally keeps it. he wants it to approach her but he decides she can wait and knows that it will start with an argument. He thinks how., then he begins why are you drinking so much, her answer to that was you do. It was a bad start to the argument he knew. She looks at him and answers straight away as she knew that he knew that she was one of them, one of the bad guys. Benjamin continues as they are running out of time his questioning her waiting for her break.
"What is it." the girl asks.
"Is what." Benjamin reply's
"Look, she says one mi note we are partying and the next minute your pinning me down and bombarding me with questions.do you think that I am the cause of everything that is happening to us or maybe you think that I am the problem. Or even more so you think that I was in the park on purpose. Come on I want to know please tell me."
"Your acting if you know something." suggests Benjamin.
"Come I want to know I was fine until the day I meet you there were no guns and nobody chasing me I was fine." Lucy shouts at Benjamin. Benjamin was now having second thoughts the girl was right but still something about her was not right. Benjamin and Lucy continue talking through the second day she answered all of Benjamin questions Benjamin still could not find any fault in her. He wanted to ken ow everything and she was happy to answer his questions. So, he says to Lucy let's start again Lucy was unhappy the second time around but answered the questions that were asked and they were pretty much the same. He asked her age in an instant she replied that the question was a rude one and refused to answer it she was now playing the game.
"Look." Benjamin says. "I am not playing games I need to know all the information. Our life s is in danger." As he continues he realizes the time. Then he continues but the girl buts in.

“I do not know anything, anything and nothing it was your company work it out for yourself.”
“why do not go back to your company and ask them.”
“I was quite happy on my own.”
“Oh, now the jokes.”
The girl catches on he was making a remark.
“It could go=f happened to anybody and the reason that I am here is that I’m here to save you.”
“Save me save me from what.”
Out of the blue as the girl is being questioned the girl looks at her watch and tells him that time is up. They are here. As soon as she finishes the sentence there a large explosion blowing the front room wall into rubble. Leaving Benjamin and herself in shell shock. Benjamin cannot move the girl had her shield on which was connected to her through her watch. Benjamin was looking around holding his ears he was just about to berserk. With the bad guys outside the girl is ready to double cross him. She had been p [art of the p [land ever since the day that they had met. Benjamin always knew that something was wrong as he always leaves his wallet in his trouser pocket and not his suit jacket. As he approaches the girl for cover he gets an electric shock from her shield. She takes a step backwards knowing that she has hurt Benjamin she was just as scared as him. Then she contacts the bad guys out side. His radios in telling them that he was was ready to collect and a little shell shocked but alive. she receives an answer.
“Okay Madame we hear you loud and clear. We will just pick him up we will be there in five minutes.”
It was Benjamin’s company and he did not know what was in him and what was on the microchip.
The girl had no idea what she was doing she had other ideas although now her boss and the team of pirates were just outside she was now protecting herself from Benjamin. Who incidentally not in a very good mood. He was trying to convince her that she was making a bad move and she was wrong and he was right. Benjamin believes that he can escape he needs his computer as all eyes and guns are on him he walks to the kitchen and retrieves the computer. As Benjamin was being approached he quickly asks the computer a few questions.
“computer can you find a way down the mountain.”
The computer tells him that there is a verse in the garage. Meanwhile the girl is distracting the bad guys Benjamin realizes what she was doing she was doing. As Benjamin waits to be blown apart

He moves out of sight. The computer is still talking.
"You can go there now as it will be safe for exactly half a minute."
"Okay computer thanks you."
As he makes his way to the garage he feels the lucks sorrow. Benjamin does not want to go without the girl he wants to send her a message but there are too many people out there. He can hear her mind she wants him to save himself. But he wants to save her he gets the message.
He leaves the garage and the mountain on a space bike just as the bad guys try by blowing the lodge up.
Even though Benjamin was saved by Lucy in Benjamin eyes it did not change anything he knew that his boss on the other side of the line had got her. He kind of felt disappointed but was not upset by any means. I was dreaming in the dream, I was asking her to come with me but she kept on denying me. I was disappointed, as the bad guys had been bombing place to place I made my way to a garage to escape everyone I was believing that the relationship with Lucy was now over. In the morning, I had awoken I jumped in to the space bike, roof down. I could still hear the echoes of the explosions through my mind. As I revved up the engines I was a little bit upset, although I was happy also just to get away from them and I was luckily that I was not dead. It was damaging my mind with every thought. The girl was inside of the company by her own accounts and chose to stay there. I did not know why. I was looking for a conversation with my comp [utter as I attached him to the bikes dash board.
"Engines." I spoke.
The engine came on. "Destination and maps". I continued to speak to it, I wanted to go to the woods I felt safer there.
"open garage door." The computer complied, I was on my way again. Strangely some had happened to start with in fact it was almost straight away the computer spoke out heavy fire to the right I had be found yet again all most instantaneously the computer spoke out again his words were brace yourself, shields up one hundred per cent. There was loads of them whatever was in that chip must be very important to them. I put the space verse into gear as I drove past them the bike was taking damage and buy the time that I had got past them NY shield were no longer there the computer was all so hit and malfunctioning as I disconnected it so it could repair itself. I was lucky enough not to be blown out of the sky. I checked the damages again this time by vision and without the use of the computer. I had been hit three or four-time s

that all I could see. but with the shields on it looked like I had avoided any serious damage. I was back on my route to nowhere I could not stop thinking about the girl like I said before that I knew that there was something about her. I needed to call my boss who I n=-knew was already the bent bad guy. I needed to know if the girl was safe. But infect I knew that she was safe as I could feel her this time around I was doing the setting up, I was going to make an approach. Mind you it might be easier if I just let them just come to me. it seemed that they could find me anywhere. Maybe I would surprise them. I had my thought but I was stupid enough to contact them again. That would be the space federal euro. In other terms, the company. Basically, the police. I put the bike in automatic then closed my eyes I was tied but I did not sleep I just sat in the seat it was smooth and made of leather as I told the computer to adjust the seat as I flew looking for a destination I was laid back and relaxed as it was a peaceful time for now.

I was out of danger for now at least I thought I was, all the thought of the girl had dispersed and the only thing that bothered me now was my boss.

For some stage reason, he was never in I wanted to why and when he was he would lie. Believing that I was believing him.

He was full of excuses, I needed to see the future, I closed my eyes trying to think in an instant I was in another mind this happened quickly as I was just closing my mind.

It was an old friend before our world on earth he was a preacher he claimed that he was a holy man.

And he had been to all kind of places before I chose to disown him he I had to admit that he was hand full when it came to verse and prayer. I did not have time for him aaaaand unshed him out of my mind.

I was hoping that he would stop, with all of it, with everything, I had not come to him to repent. But for an idea to save the girl.

I did not ask him if he was holy I already knew and when I went to question him slowly he managed to twist the conversation around he was now questioning me.

We sat and discussed many things but there was nothing that he could tell me that I did not already know.

When I had opened my eyes, I knew more than I could off perceived I was trying to push the thought is that he gave me away. it was a hard thing to do.

Who was he I asked myself. And how did I manage to find him. He had one more question for me he had asked what wryer my true intentions.
I answered the first question then the second there was nothing else to say. He left me a vision.
Then I asked him another question and again he did not answer he sent me another vision.
The first vision was of the girl Lucy she was holding me at gun point. The second vision there was nothing but in the third vision the images that I receive d were all fuzzy and I could not make heads or tail over it. but I did sense that it was her. It ws unaus formed to close my eyes when I did not need some form I-=of information I was waiting for my mind to travel within a few moments I was there I had travel up through my mind and into his he was telling the truth. He was ahoy he said he was. There was no need to raise any more questions. As I slowly came back to my mind I opened my eyes,
I told the computer to send a message to our headquarters but again I had the same problem as before the computer did not recognise the orders. I was not sure whether he had heard me so I gave the command again and again nothing. I was thinking now that something else was wrong and the computer was a part of the plan and it was also in on the deal. I decided to question it.
I started. “computer is you damaged.” There ws no reply.
I continued again “who is in control of you.”
It gave me a reply “I am.” It told me.
Then I asked it “why are you ignoring my orders.”
The computer refused to answer the only other thing that I could think that was possible wrong was that someone had hacked into him. Benjamin give s him some knew orders to fix him. Then after wards Benjamin continue s to question him in the end he still gets nothing from it and takes the computer off the bikes bash board.
Benjamin need is a space verse and is hoovering low enough to find a car show room even though the car had specialized equipment he could re set the computer and there would be a lesser chance on the street cameras picking them up. He lands the space bike and finds a space car. He fixes the computer into the dashboard turning it off so that it avian get use d to its new environment. Within a few minutes Benjamin has the computer talking to him. As he calls himself and the computer down. He thinks that his in a safe place there was not many people around and the roads were pretty much empty. Benjamin wants

to take him and the computer to a safer place. He sits down in the car thinking where they could go. After a conversation with his computer all he could find out that there was a homing chip but the computer did not know where. The computer explains that s is why we keep on getting caught. Benjamin asks the computer how long did you know about this there was no answer. He takes the computer off the dash board again turning it off knowing that it is his only friend apart from the girl and drive off out of the town. When Benjamin get stop the forest he gets out of the car and tells the computer that he is going to bury it with his friends. Benjamin gets out of the verse with the computer in one hand as the computer is still on he is questioning Benjamin behaviour Benjamin opens his trunk after telling the computer to open the truck the computer compiles it seemed convenient to walk through in to a place that he would remember. he finds s a small lake. He takes off his clothes and stands on the river bank he closes his eyes as he removes his shoes and wades off into with the computer and a trowel.

As Benjamin dives into the water taking the trowel with him he finds the bottom and starts digging the computer gives him enough wait to sink to the bottom it was not that deep but deep enough to hide a computer. He grabs his breathe as he comes to the top he had to be quick.

As he come up out of the lake he says to himself." the computer is dead and buried."

He swims back to the sandy banks. And returns himself to his car. But does not get in as he dries himself off. Before getting into the car. Benjamin continues the conversation with himself

"Who is the computer going to double cross next first the girl and now me."

He closes his eyes and take himself all the way back he could clearly everything that had happened he was watching images of himself but nothing of the microchip. Due to the fact of having an argument with the only system that would recognise what was on the chip and on top of that Benjamin was running out of places to hide. At least this time he knew when he had been double crossed. First the girl and now my computer. Benjamin believes that the girl is no more as he had left her on top of the mountain. I was now in the country side not knowing where I was going. I was still receiving images of what had happen into my mind it was like having shell shock.

The images where so subline I had to stop and spend some time in hard should at the side of the country lane. As the thoughts of the images that I was receiving were so powerful I had passed out. As I awoke I crawled out of the car I could not stand up still half-dressed I was not sleep walking a such but something similar. I had stepped into the middle of the road. Then into a small field I was looking for something or even more so they were looking for me. I had totally woken up about a hundred feet from my car. Feeling that my eyes wryer heavy it was like I was on moonshine. It really was it was like I was drunk. I was without my mind. My small journey continued as I then found myself in the middle of the road again except I was on my back. Not knowing how I got there, there was no traffic and all I could hear was the sound of the small bushes blowing in the wind I was going crazy.

The worst thing about the last thought was that it had no answer, I had lost it I was now going insane. The only thing that was saving me ws the thought of the girl. As I made it back to my car I managed to get back into the car but I was still half asleep not knowing the dreams and the visions that I had there was no possible way that I was going to drive the car. I was to lethargic I decided to wait there until the morning, I was about to pass out again then I did. I was out for about seven or eight hours when I woke up. For some strange reason, I was woken by a stag I was not sure wearer it was a dream or if what I could see was real. I had not mentioned it before but it seemed strange and I then realized that I had the dream before when I was little except in the dream when I was a child I was standing in the road opposite the stag. Looking at it as it was looking for me. I did not know what the actual dream mint. Even though the dream had been recurring I was trying to think what it mints, properly nothing.

As I got board of thinking about the dream and put it aside I was quickly awoken back in the car. Not knowing that I had been sleep walking and with no computer I was on my own. But knowing that I had been trapped without any knowledge and whoever was on the other side had also trapped my best friend. I leant bac k over the seat looking for the computer then remembering that I had buried it in the lake. I shifted into the driver's seat I was thinking that maybe. As I threw the thought of the dream away and put the rest of the thoughts of the dream aside I was quickly awoken in the car. As gore the computer I had completely forgotten where I had buried it. my mind was in way of confusion. I could not make up my mind if I wanted the c computer if should dig it up again and

CHAPTER NINE

possibly re wire it I thought hard about this I even got out of the car and thought about it as I walked around it, laying on its bonnet and hugging it like a girl. I finally figured it out I was on my own.
The computer and the company were hiding things it was obvious to me now, I was beginning to think that I was not just brought back to find the microchip and the girl but I was being set up but why was the question. I was running out of places to hide and I was not sure if I was still being followed and when I did find a place to hide the bad guys always seemed to find me.

he was on his own and he had the chips he knew that it would not belong before they would find him. He was tempted to throw the microchips away but they had something on them and I wanted to know what. I needed to find out why there were following him and why the trying to kill him. More to the fact what was on the microchip.
As he drove back from the forest and into the countryside I was half awake it was the same kind of feeling as before I was thinking now that I had been poisoned but I had not eaten anything for a while and the wine from the party up in the mountain had passed through me days ago. This was not good I was passing in and out of=f consciousness I could not put the car on auto pilot as I had no computer I needed to take another break though he had just had one nothing would work in the car unless it had the computer I was screwed. In the end, I got out of the car cussing and cursing and screaming just a little bit of road rage. I will not tell you exactly what I said but it was not nice I gave it a mouth full and started walking. It was weird that there was no other traffic about the roads that I was on was silent as I was checking my gun I had half a magazine left in it. leaving the car was a bad decision I knew that it was because it p [layer on my mind. Somewhere down the line. I wanted to turn back but my consciousness had got the better of me and I continued walking. I had looked up at the sky the first time in ages I could tell by the clouds that there was a storm coming. I left the road and headed to the nearest trees I was thin king if the weather does not get me the wolfs in the forest will. After an hour of walking in the wood I made it back to the road it felt a lot safer. Except there was no cover and I was still vulnerable. I looked up at the sky again for the second time in my actual life I knew my soul was looking for something. the night was cold there was no need for the computer now even though that I missed it as he was my guide. There was still no traffic and if there was I would problem hitch a lift. Not a sound it was not getting any easier. The wolfs were out I could clearly hear them. this walk was not going be easy. As I was walking all I could hear was the wind it was like it was talking to me but I refused to follow it was trying hard to drear me in to a direction on this occasion I had one as I managed to stay on the path but where I was going I did not know I had no destination. As I kept on walking Tithe weather changed for the better I could see a lot better and I could see that there was going to be

another storm as the thunder and lightning came down I found myself clinging on to a tree holding on for dear life.
The thunder storm was vast it seemed to start in the distance one mo0ment the next it was right on top of me. also, even more so one moment I could walk the next I was hiding amount the trees all over again. On this occasion, the tree that I had hid under was struck and I had been electrocuted. It happened so fast but I expected something. when I had awoken from the shock I felt sexy it was a different feeling than before I closed my eyes picking myself off the floor I continued to walk as I made my way back out of the small wood and up a bank on to the main road again. I was struck again I could not believe it this time I was blown off my feet and laid on the road like a dead turkey as I rolled around in pain I guess that it was bad luck. I know now I would have been better in the car. I knew now but I kept on walking it was apostolate rocketing it down, first hail stone then on top of that, hard fast rain the face stinging type. It was like a dream I had to ask myself to wither it was real or just my imagination. I was being driven mad. I called out as I was walking along, speaking to myself I was chanting a song I was chanting like I was in the chain gang except there was only me that was doing the chanting to the rhythm of the rain.

I was on my way to the nearest town as I walked closer towards my destination it was getting nosier. I could hear the the towns traffic as I came out of the woods and off the main road. I could see the city's lights easily. But I was not out of danger yet infect I was probably walking into danger. I could stumble out off the road and woods and slowly find some normal streets. I was not feeling too comportment in exerting the town when I got into the town I found myself a cheap hotel. As I walked through the door entering the Maun reception and ringing the bell on the counter. I stood there for a minute or two then some greasy fat bloke came walking in, he approached me.
"Hello what can we do for you this evening."
"A room." I asked
"Yeah we have a few."
I put some credits on the counter. He replied.
"You do not have to pay me yet wait until the morning."
I told him to take the money as I did not like debt so he did.
"that's room 44." he said handing me the keys, I thanked him and went up to know what was my room for the night.

I laid on the bed to tired just to fall asleep too tired of the worry of being found however it was probably safer being in a poor run-down hotel as it drew less attention. I was thinking about everything that had happened and I was still concerned about the girl Lucy who looks like she had double crossed me.
Going back to the room it was comfortable one and I was at home I needed a shower so I got undressed and jumped in.
"Dam." I was speaking to myself. "no hot water, I should have expected that. Being in the run-down place."
I was clumsy not to native=cue that I was caring a spy with me. it did not surprise me that she was a double agent. I was busy grilling myself for being so stupid. Anyway, I had both microchip both with me I was going back to base I had already tried to contact them but as I picked up the phone but just as I was tapping in the last number I lost it and hesitated and put the phone down as I thought something was wrong. I took the phone and as I did it fell open in my hands.

It basically fell apart in my hands typically foreign rubbish, as I took a good look at it and I was trying to piece it together again but I was getting know where I found a device in it, it looked like a homing device I was not shocked but knew why one of the reasons that I was in constants danger. I was thinking what else that I could be carrying. The chip was quite small so I knew why I had missed it I guess it could have happened to anyone it just so happened to be me, understanding the circumstances. I closed my eyes fiddling around with it sometimes feeling is better than sight. Eventually I forced my way in the mechanism. Only to rip it apart and destroy it as I ripped and dislodged from its circuit board, so they could no longer follow him.
It was night time I was laying on my bed it was not the most comfortable bed s that I had ever slept on. But it seemed safe enough. I had decided to take a late evening walk you know new town new faces just to take a looks around town and to check the place out. As I walked through the run-down hotel corridors I put my ear on a cold wooden panel and tried to listen there was nothing. I then walked toward as another door facing east I tried the door handle but it was locked. I could not hear anything then as I pulled my head away it opened I jumped backwards in shock. Then behind me a voice.

“what are you doing.”
I needed a quick excuse.
“I thought that I heard something next door. It sounded like a cry for help.”
“do not be stupid the only thing in that room next door is my dog. And I did not hear it bark.”
I was not sure whether I should have apologised for being noisy. I continued down the corridor to a balcony I needed a smoke so I pulled the packet that I had in my jacket pocket. It seemed safer out on the balcony than in the hotel bedroom, I was sitting down, as I took another pull of the cigarette I was relaxed I closed my eyes waiting for images the vision to start but nothing I was falling asleep at last. I could finally get some rest, I was there for most of the night I was dreaming of looking in to the night and for some strange reason looking for a way out an escape.
Just incise anything was to happen I was still on the balcony as I awoke but there was another balcony properly leading to a dining area I could have done with a beer and some food. I could smell it, it was below me to one side. As I looked, it seemed to be another escape route another way-out side. The only other way out of the place was down I did not mind heights. But I knew but I knew if I was to fall that far I was going to receive some definite damage at the least a broken ankle. I was prepared.
When I had finished the smoke that I had, I put it out in an ash tray polity. I was feeling no better than when I had started. Then I was ready I needed my computer I had not completely forgotten about him. And I’m sure that because he has human thoughts it was still thinking of me buried or not. I had to go back to find him if I could remember where I buried it. I needed the computer because I wanted to dismantle it as I believed that it had some kind or possible a homing chip in him but again something should be left alone. But however, it was one way in thinking that I could find out exactly what the company were planning to do and what they were planning to do to me. I took both the microchips out of my jacket, holding them in my hand, as I pulled another phone from my jacket as I opened the phone as I exchanged the chips I was surprised that the chip fitted I now had my computer back so I could leave it where it was, for now. As I place d the chip into the phone the knowledge that I was just about to receive did not come from the phone as such. But it entered me through my eyes I could see everything, plans, documents, escape documents, they were

all plans of the worlds future. you name it in could see it, it was there I had plans for things that in did not know existed and did not understand.
As the knowledge of the chip streamed in the me I could see clearly that there was going to be another war so the ears around the earths where no longer going to be at peace. But because od=fan certain things such as assassins the work our world was going to crumble. The knowledge that I had received was at its up most. I was telling myself that I had no reason not to believe this. I was asking who else knows this apart of myself. I could understand now why they wanted the microchips back. I had begun to think that know I had received the knowledge and I could walk in but not out. After I had seen enough I removed the chip from my phone I had to agree that I had received an extraordinary message that I had just received according to the micro=chip it could only be used once. The knowledge was in me now I was now their target.

Which explains why I'm was being chased. The company must of thought that I had already read the chip but I had not until now that the plans were in me the chase was back on. As I went to disown the phone down the hotel toilet I went to remove the chip but the chip was not there. Then for some reason unexplained my car keys keys began to flash taking into mind that I had walked twelve-mile s to get to the hotel. I was a little bit suspicious I waked to the curtains in the bedroom and slowly looked outside. Someone was trying to contact me. as I had the phone it only could be the computer. I walked slowly and quickly down the hotel corridors towards the steps outside into the car park. I walked toward the verse, when I got there I looked through the window, no driver I looked in and to my surprise the computer was there everything in place as I leant on the body of the car I could clearly see that the computer was back. I opened the door and all the other doors with my keys. The computer was there. I was happy I picked it up pushing it into the dash board, it was like having an old ashamed car stereo his systems must of corrected itself it had woken up we were back in business.
Once the excitement was over I took the computer out of the car and back in to the hotel with me quietly upstairs. I was in my room again looking for a connection just to find out what was going on. There was none I was upset, but excited. I was happy as I had my computer back. He was my best friend. I placed it down gently on the bed room table

after removing a few other things nothing that mattered. I finally could relax I was lying on the bed I could finally close my eyes. And I felt a little safer as I had the computer for company. Even though he was not plugged in it did not occur to me that I could have left him in the car wanted to put him back into the dashboard.

In the first instance, the first time I met the girl in the park I had got a good night's sleep as I awoke I woke up with the computer on my chest. I must have grabbed it while I was asleep.

I was not ready to awake just yet, as I put the computer down on the bed beside me. I was looking at the bed side table. I rolled over onto my side and went back to sleep, stupidly leaning on the tv control. The tv came on it was loud as I tried to turn it down in a hurry as I awoke even more. I could not get back to sleep as I turned it down as I was now awaking but wanted to sleep it made no difference. As I turned off the tv I lent on it again turning it on again I must have lent on it hard. As I was fighting to find the remote control as it flicked from station to station and finally the news. To my surprise I ws on the news at first, I did not believe it but it was true. Then it hit me they had found me again.

CHAPTER TEN

I went to my bedroom window I could hear police sirens they were constant throughout the night I knew straight away that the ass hole down stairs had sold me out. I grabbed the computer, while locking the bed room door and turning the the shower on as a decoy, as well as the tv, turning it up full. I opened the window and stepped on to the ledge I had already planned my escape. It was a long way down there but I thought what's a broken ankle but again it was a long way down there I was walking on the ledge but I could only go so far. I could see that there was another building close as I put the com putter into my jacket to protect from the jump. I was telling myself that I could do it and it was possible. I was also trying to tell myself that it was not that far down. I made a leap for it I landed right on the d=edge of another wall and then I could leap again, time was not on my side. I was balanced on another wall on one leg. As I pulled the other leg on to the brick wall I was safe, well I thought I was there was still ten feet to go. I could see the wall it was poorly made even though it looked short it was not it was taller or longer than I had anticipated. I took my chance I made my way along the wall looking for a safer place to land I was walking along a wall making the next part of my escape. I knew w that I was bng followed I could hear the hotel manager shouting from the other room. I walked along the wall like a pussy cat there was a couple of drain pipes I ws not sure whether they would hold me then I was on a roof I was hanging on to things I was now thinking that there was no way out apart from letting go, as I seemed to be moving up rather than down in the end I was in the dark not knowing whether I was moving up but wanting to be moving down not knowing where I was going to land luckily there was another roof and finally the floor luckily they had stopped at the hotel window I had made the final a jump down. I made my way way to the front of the hotel with my car keys and the computer tucked in my jacket. As I came around the front the p [police cars were there waiting for me infect they were everywhere. I pulled up my hooded top to compile myself. I clicked the car keys avoiding the the police and got into my car. Avoiding contacting anyone. A s I clicked theca keys and opened the car doors, as I pulled the computer out of my jacket placing it into the dashboard. I did not know how I did it but I did. I managed to get back into the car and the police let me go on my way. It was good that they did not recognise me. the police were everywhere I thought that I was in the clear but the fun was just about to start.

As I was driving away I past the girl and her henchmen, I was not sure if the girl had recognised me although I saw her clearly, up front was a road block. It was a little bit obvious that the road block was for me. I put the brakes on to stop to give me time to think. As my future now looked dim as I looked in the rear-view mirror I could clearly see there was police behind me.

If I was to reverse it would be a little obvious I had no choice but to approach the road block. I was keeping my cool as I reversed and leant in to the back seat to pick up the computer pushing it to the dash board.it spoke to me.

"how are you." It said

I told the computer that there was a road block ahead which was the quickest way out of here."

It continued. "all system on."

I continued. "there is a road block ahead which is the quickest way out of here, safely which is the quickest route out of town."

The computer gave me some new directions because I had turned the car around it raised suspicion I had no choice for now but to floor the pedals and head in the other direction I did not know how I did it but I did I was back in the clear for now. As I had nowhere to go as I had run out of hiding places it seemed to me at that point that I was as bad as bad guys. And as the bad guys seemed to be able to find me anywhere even though I had some pretty court safe houses and the fact that they had found everyone it could no longer be the the girl. So, it had to be me. I decided to speak to the computer.

"Computer I asked scan me for a devise." I asked.

There was no answer so I said it again.

"Computer can you scan me for s microchip."

This time he answered,

"yes, I can, please close your eye."

My reptile to the computer was "is that it."

The computer replied" pretty much so Benjamin."

In an instant, I knew the bug was in me and not in the computer or anywhere else. I knew now that's was the reason that the bad guys had kept on finding me, over and over. Where inside of me I did not know but I was just about to find out. I needed frank he awes an old friend it was my only option the last of my friends even though we did not get on I had one chance and one chance only. He was the only person that I knew that would understand. And he was the only person who could remove the chip without killing me. I did not have to think twice about

this decision that I was just abou6t to make. I tapped the address into my computer. Hoping that the car would take me there to his address and home. I knew that already that I was being followed I did not want to tell him for the thought of him sending me away.
I told the computer to send him a message but the computer told me that there was no answer. I tried to call him over the intercom but again there was no answer.
I was thinking that maybe it was a mistake. I was worried as frank was normally in and if he was he would normally pick up and answer his messages. Mind you it was Sunday according to him then day of rest. Even though by the time I got there it would have been Monday so I did not see the problem. I was worried as frank has not picked up the phone. I told my computer to try again, I was running out of ideas and I ws running out of time I said to myself and to the com putter exactly what I was thinking I need frank, I tried once more but there was no answer at that point.
I had to make a session should I continue or should I give in for now. Untried once more even knowing that I was not going to get an answer. I eventually left a message that I would be in the area around lunch time and if he was in I would like to join him. Weather he liked it or not.
I tapped in his address into the computer system, as I took my hands off the steering wheel and relaxed leaving the computer to do the driving and closed my eyes.

As I drifted in and out of consciousness slowly approaching my destination realizing that this was the last c hanker of escape. And knowing that frank was the only other answer that I ha d and that made sense to everything that had happened he was level headed and ws reasonable but I could not trust him in fact I could not trust anyone, however I was just about to find out. The computer woke me up as I awoke the computer told me we were within a mile of the destination and told me it was the right time to wake up and adjust. When I had got to the destination I was now totally awake. My car was parked right outside his estates gates I told my computer to hack into his computer and open his gates since the computer could not open the gates by hacking into the other computer system However it managed to get me the gates code. I got out of the car kn*owing that I was properly on camera I knew that it made no difference they knew that I was* there I took the coordinates and pushed them into a small computer pad. The gates opened I got into the car and slowly drove it up to the next set of gates it was about half a mile and again I went through the same routine first asking the computer to hack and then after receiving the coordinates. As got out of the car again and punched them in to the computer pad. I haws happy that I had made it, the gates opened again as I put my foot down slowly down on the accelerator and drove in. it was a long way up to his drive and his actual home ws massive. Just as I was parking up the computer gave me the address. I wanted to throw the computer away. I pulled up outside nobody was or came out of the building to greet me. I was sup rid=seed as due to the size of the mansion and it looked extremely rich. I was looking around as we were in the future it seemed old fashioned as other building that I have been and seen were all extremely futuristic this was taking me back in time.

It was like walking back in time like living in the past, who wants to live in the future, as I closed the cars systems and got out of the car as it told me that I had reached my destination. As I walked hastily to the front door of the home. I knocked on the door a couple of times not knowing what the answer would be I now was hope full that he would be there after a long wait he finally came to the doors we greeted each other.

"Benjamin".

"it is so good to see you." I said

"it's been a long time how long, how are things please come in." Frank insisted.

We continued to talk as we walked through the long corridors of the large building.

"so." Frank begins again. "what brings you this way."

"it is hard to explain do you have a few hours."

Franks reply was welcoming again I began to tell him everything exactly how it was happening and how it happened. And exactly how what was to come I did not have a long time and time was running thin.

As I continued and began again after a pause I continued telling how I believed that my body had been bugged somewhere and somehow. I

had worried him it was not my intentions as I was worried already myself. He explained that he could find out where the chip was but he could not remove it by himself and he was not certain and continued that there was a high risk that he might be wrong and the chip might not even be where he believed. As he was talking I butted in as he was trying to explain I was telling him now that I had been here he was now in danger and it was a must that he should leave his home as the chip was on me. it was obvious that soon the bad guys were going to appear. I begged him to come with me it was lucky he finally agreed. As we continued to speak he said that he might know w man that could fix it. Frank also said that the bug was not in my stomach as I predicted but it was in my eye my right eye. So, I was finally getting somewhere, we were both ready to leave I could feel them they were close. I told him to tap the destination into the computer and he did. I kept on talking to him as we maundered into a flying position, I had to question him just to make sure it was him and I was not talking to a robot or anybody else. As we spoke I was trying to tell him that I had been set up right from the start I explained to him earlier I did not think he wanted to hear it again so I stayed quiet.
As we were flying above his woods and over mountains heading towards the city I was feeling a lot better I think it was franks presents and that I knew were the chip was, but as I thought about it I was beginning to feel more and more ill. I told frank he said as he understood.
I was feeling uneasy so I told the computer to put its foot down I needed to get to the destination fast, the computer hit high speed. I wanted to get there fast again in told the computer to speed up. I could not even if I wanted to take over the flying as I was now feeling poorly. I continued to speak to frank just to keep myself from passing out.
"Frank according to the computer we will be there in fifteen minutes."
"What's the address."
Frank had passed out due to the speed of the verse, I could not be bothered to help him wake I just felt that I should not wake him as he looked comfortable asleep, so I asked my computer I pulled the verse over, we were about twenty feet above the ground, that's twenty feet above the actual road the computer woke up frank. I told the computer to slow down and within a minute he came around just as I was passing out I never got the chance to finish what I was trying to say to him.

“Hay wake up.” frank said slapping me gently around the face. I could feel him move my head, I was drooling a little, as he wiped the side of my mouth and woke me up.
“Finally,” he said as he was happy to see me awake.
“We are not at the destination since you did not give me the address.” The address Benjamin said err yes it the pharmaceutical on. he was inter erupted that’s the computer Benjamin begins give me the address. The reply by the computer was “I do not know the reply just the address just the name and directions”.
Benjamin tells the computer to give them to him the computer does as he is requested. the computer begins to resist Benjamin rises his voice “give them to me.” the computer complies.
In the process frank pulls out a pen out of his pocket he is usually caring a knife and scribbles down the notes that Benjamin s reply was sorry I did not feel so good frank answer to that was I do not either. Frank replies “I know that would be the microchip it is going to work on your mind and its seems your insides.
“What do you mean.”
“It is the microchip I know I created it you’re on the right tracks, first you will vomit then you will lose your appetite so that you cannot outback what you thaw out then you will suffer a dry mouth and if you are really persistent in fighting those tree systems you will find that you will have a wet mouth as your body will start to preserve the opposite of what you think and so on and so on. He continued that I may choke in my sleep.
My future was not going to be a nice one, the things that were just spoken about were not nice. My politeness was killing me. it was all getting to much for me as I Benjamin had reach out of the window and vomited. It seemed that the closer I was getting g to the factory the worst I would feel. I was just hoping that I had the enough strength to make it.
I was speaking to my computer “we must get there and get there fast.” The computer spoke back we were or looked like we were on level points.
“We will be there in five minutes hold on.”
Benjamin was on his way to being fixed, a few minutes later they arrived the computer was right. Frank introduces Benjamin him to his scientific friend and doctor.
“I already know why you are here I have been waiting for you.”
“Good, get the chip out of me.”

"Wait."
"Wait for what."
"I need to know what kind of chip I am moving."
Benjamin wanted to know what kind of chip he was removing.
Benjamin was getting more and more unsettled and the doctor was trying to say that he shoes=old settle down before he decided to report the operation.
In the microchip, the doctor found that it was also an explosive and the doctor made Benjamin aware of that of course Benjamin flip out about as well. As he was operating the doctor continuously told Benjamin to keep still as what he was removing was extremely delicate.
#benjami9n did as he was told. As he removed the chip from his eye with the special equipment Benjamin shout as he sits up I am free. As the scientist disregards the microchip Benjamin tells him to stop.
What the doctor says.
Wait Benjamin says and continues
Give me the chip
Why he says if you drop this baby we may all die
I am not going to drop it between you and me and you I want you to tell me what is on it.
If I told you that it was a map of the the last whole war which exists in our children's future, it is was to be controlled by the plans of the chips there would be no more peace and the chip hold s the answers to it so what would happen if it was destroyed.
I will leave you to understand it if you can, and I will leave you the thought if it…
Benjamin interrupts.
"What."
The scientist loses his temper and Benjamin continues, "I have the chip."
The scientist continues there would "no chip", he continued." Without this chip, there would be no peace."
"without no chip, there would be no answers."
Frank continue that know that he had helped me that he should leave. I greed and he left.
Benjamin sits down, he wants to know what's on the chip, even though he knows what he has just been told.
"The microchip fits into your computer that's all I can help you with the___14 doctor shouts at Benjamin and frank grabs Benjamin by his

arm. As I now know what had happened to the message and microchip I wanted to head Back to headquarters if I could find the address.

As I drove and drove fast o knew that my boss was setting me up right from the very start everything that had happened was from right from the start it was his fault I was reading it, this evenings paper that I had just brought form the paper boy as we were leaving the town centre with the chip in my hand I placed it genteelly on the dash board.
I moved through the traffic fast as we were leaving a town to another town I was welding the chip the microchip in my hand I had a little bag in it was the microchip. I placed it genially on the dashboard. I did not know who my name was. But within an hour I would find out my real name. and my future, it would be known to my soul again. As I shifted the car into to great again I ripped, dodging the the traffic lights and pedestrians. I was dodging in and out of traffic until I was on the main road the fast lane was mine. The computer gave me some music but it was classical. The computer compiled.
As I drew nearer and nearer to our destination I stopped the car and told frank to get o0ut he did not understand. Until I explained that he could be in danger of his life, eventually he caught on and stepped outside, as he did he asked me the stupid question if he could be my back up. I explained that I had back up already and that was that. He seemed up set I asked him if he would like to die he said no. the I said stay put.
I said to him if he could stay in the car it would help he ws happy to do that.
I told him that I would come back to him, his reply was that he would be missing a lot pf action, he persisted to continue the conversation. In the end, I was getting nothing. I told frank that I was walking the rest of the way to the house and I told frank that I was leaving him behind If he liked it or not. As we drew nearer to the destination, I stopped the car and told frank, He did not understand. He continued," look frank I have some serious business that I have to attend too do you understand. There will be nothing if I stay here. I would be about a mile away ad that's all."
After a little more debating I agreed to leave frank in the car and headed my way on foot before I left I told him not to touch anything as my computer and verse could be a little centime natal. I kept the keys to make sure that he would not drive off and if I was lucky he would

not hot wire it, he was quite clever in those terms. As I left I called out to him in a joking manor.
"I have the keys just remember."
As I was now on foot and I could hear the last comments that frank spoke which were.

"I will catch you later Mr cool."

CHAPTER ELEVEN

I had the microchip on or in me that I was going to use to bribe my way in. the only other problem was security I knew now to destroy the chip its slightest knock or being handled heavily could force it to disrupt. I mean if I was to throw it down hard enough it would explode and all the knowledge on it would be lost. It could be better for everybody on this planet at least they would not know that a nuclear war was being set up. Through the company, through the worlds computer systems. I did not want to believe eat but it was true. I was talking to myself as I was walking. I said something like
"why mew why was I left with the chip in me."
I was thinking if they knew that there was one of the chips in me and I was thinking that why if they knew that they had set me free but also sent me to meet the girl and the rest of it why would they send me half way around the city. If they wanted me to make a run for it to make it easier for them or perhaps they did not know, but in all this time I must ask the question how did they keep on finding me as all the places that I had hid in were closure. I was thinking about the girl she also had the chip which I had taken it matched mine. I was just about to find out what was going to happen.
As I was walking I pressed the button on my jacket and within a second a helmet and visor appeared. I could see in to the dark and everything the gear that I was wearing was infer red
"cool." I thought. Then I told it to go to night vision it did. I could see everything there was weird stuff, information it looked like maps of some sort. As I approached the mouse there was a guard I could see him clearly and the helmet that I was wearing spoke to me tell me that it was safe to approach him as he was un armed. I manged to stroll past

him without him noticing me. although as I past guard after guard I was beginning to think that it was a little bit too easy any way I was beginning to think that they were expecting me. I was thinking that if they already knew that I was here I might as well give myself up. But just as I was going to shout to call the dogs, I felt something in my jacket pocket to my surprise it was a lavatory pass. I took it out of the pocket and looked at it, photograph and everything. I approached the guard.
“Hello, I am late for an appointment.”
The guard was just about to ask me some questions I butted in.
“do you know who I am.”
I continued to grill him until he broke and told me where to go he continued up on to the first floor down the corridor and to the right then down the corridor to the left then take a right and up the steps to the second floor then down the corridor and it’s the door on the right. I thanked him not being able to ask him again for direction as I totally did not understand where I was supposed to go so I played by ear again. I thanked him and walked in as I found the density action the room I was being expected I walked through the lavatory door and was greeted as I zapped in with my id card.
“At last Benjamin, I have been waiting for you.”
“You have.” I answered.
He continued “You have something of mine.”
“I do and what would that be” I said.
“hand me the microchip. I know that I have something of yours.”
The girl walks out.
She shouts” Benjamin.”
Benjamin tries to resist but there is too much pressure even more so knowing that the girl is there again and trying to think weather he is being set up again.
The company continues. Hand me the chip and the girl and you can go free.”
Benjamin does not but it. the companies pushed s a phaser into the girl.
The girl tells the guy with the gun that she is trying. He nudges her again beaming already knows.
“you double crossing bitch.” He says grabbing her.
“They made me do it.”
Benjamin pushes her of him and take a couple of steps backwards the bad guys continues.

“Give me the microchip. You do not want to know but you are dealing with powers that you would not understand. I planted the chip in you sixty years ago and now I want it back Benjamin.”
Benjamin is now losing his mind trying to calculate Benjamin is now on his knees trying to fight his mind as he his traveling backwards in time everybody on and in the station, are watching him
“You cannot beat it Benjamin you are not strong enough.” The girl says hold in and pointing a gun at him. Telling him that if he does not produce the chip within the next few second s she would kill him. Benjamin does not buy it and still refuses to give in. the microchip is still stuck in Benjamin but he still has the girls he pushes across the floor, the girl un clicks her pistol and steps around him to pick it up.
“that’s better Benjamin you may stand up.”
Benjamin stands the company continues with laughter and compliments and these words s were said. “you see how powerful we all are.”
“Now where is the other one I will tell you why I need it because swear] n both of the chips are brought tighter there will be a reaction a chemical reaction of destruction and that’s what the people on this planet deserve. There will be a total mass of reincarnation of everything, and I will have the world.”

At that point for some strange reason the slide me a weaponeer both chips were being put together I had the other one in me and it looked like the only way of getting it out of me was my death.
Suddenly frank walks in. “what are you doing here I told you to stay put.”
“I thought that you needed a little bit of support. You know back up.”
“You take the girl I all go after the chip.”
As I sent an array of bullets in the direction of the bad guys. I got some hell fire back if the chips were put tighter there would be a chance of destruction but I was sure that they needed a third chip and it was in me. I was still wait g to find out why the chip was planet in me after some gun fire and hell fire I was taking them out easily they were dropping like flies. The girl, ws right behind me I still could not trust her. She was telling me to leave to get out of the building yelling at me like she was crazy.
“if you do not leave now they will kill you.
That to me was a suggestion that things were going to get a little rougher. I did not have a chance to play along with the girl like I said

before she was un trust worthy. I did not have time time to play lovey dove with her. I pushed her of my back as she was behind me as we both took on cannon fodder.
I shouted at her trying with mine hand her emotions.
"One minute you're with me the next you are not. Whose side are you on."
She knelt as all the cannon fire smashed her surroundings apart.
"I'm yours Benjamin." She shouted as she knelt with both arms stretched out wards as she fired her weaponeers, bringing her targets down. I could see straight away that she was going to sacrifice herself. I did not have the time to play levy dove with this girl, I pushed her off me. shouting at her" who's side are you on."
I continued "one minute you are with me the next minute you are not, stop playing games with me."
"Fine are you with me."
This was all I could say for the position that we were both in. she continued
"If you could have only believed in me."
"Come on let's do this."
She agreed, as she was armed I was too I shouted to her as we were going to take them all out.
There were bullets flying everywhere, I was going after the chip and told her, the girl was with me for a couple more minutes she was sure that she could take them out by herself as she Didi giving me enough cover to move. I could hear the bad guy as I shook up to them he was saying some like.
"You cannot do it with part of the chip just think what we could accomplish if we both brought them together."
I butted in surprising them. "call your men off and we can make a deal."
"No chance. I fell for that the first time."
Benjamin shouts across the room" but the way it's nice to be back."
Benjamin keeps an eye on the beds guy as he continues to fire upon the pirates they were hitting the deck fast but they kept on coming Benjamin was worried that he was going to run out of ammunition. And says to himself
"I'm running out of ammunition. And I am running out of ideas."
Benjamin closes his eyes putting himself in touch with his computer asking him for some back up. Then for some reason there was not a sound in the whole of the building. Then the girl drops a cartage and

the whole thing starts off all over again. Benjamin was busy asking the computer where was the chip.
"It seems to me that there are two chips which we are looking at one of them is real and the other is a fake but however they both look like the same on my system. I believe that he has gone underground." The computer replied. The computer tells Benjamin to wait the computer tells Benjamin that there is a mistake I now believe that he has gone to the top of the building he is going towards the roof.
Benjamin shouts" which one."
"I cannot be certain," the computer says.
"Can you track both chips at the same time." Benjamin shouts
"No, I cannot the computer says not unless I am in the verse."
Benjamin's car was way way down stairs buy the time he would have got there it would be too late. Benjamin calls out to the girl we have three choices one you can go back down stairs with this my computer and try and track him from there or two you can stick with me and we party on the roof or we both give up the roof thing and party down stairs underground. She replies quickly
"I'm coming with you." They both ran towards the left doors Lucy just making it as Benjamin tries to hit the first-floor button more cannon fire as the doors quickly close. Benjamin puts the lift on hold.
"if he is not up there then he s down there we need that chip okay. Are you willing to die because it might happen?"
"I'm in ill lead." Lucy says confidently.
Benjamin and Lucy begin to travel back up the tower to the top. There was very few guards and a lot quieter and nothing that they could not handle. Benjamin was worried that they did not have enough gun power as he was slowly running out of bullets.
But as it happens just by luck he was using a gun that the magazine of the beds guys the pirates fitted and as there was two dead bad guys in front of him he checked their pockets after killing them and found more magazines. He was feeling better and his confidence grew back.
As I picked up the magazine we both moved father up the building this time using the stairs.
"he could be anywhere do you think he has gone down satire I mean underground."
"The girl shouts Benjamin grabs her saying that we have enough problems as it is you do not have to tell everybody in the building that we are here."
"They already no."

"Look are being funny because this is no time to joke. Now hold your lounge."
Benjamin throws a magazine to her she locks it into her gun.
They go to room to room not knowing where he was or where the chip was taking the occasional shoulder on the way.
"we must be going in the right direction or his guards would not be here."
"how do you know."
"Because if he was close to us there would not be any body around."
"Just as Benjamin finishes the sentence there a huge explosion he shouts out to the Lucy grab my hand. We should leave his not up here and I think we would be better off going underground."
"Err yeah do you not think that you are stating the obvious."
It was too late Benjamin could not figure it out quick enough and they were both caught in the explosion as Benjamin drags her with extreme force they just make to the outside of the building there is a hole force in front of them they were doomed this time it looked killed they had lost but as the building fell there was a lot of dust and it cover them and it blocked the pirates vision as they knew that Benjamin knew as the dust dispersed Benjamin and the girl disappeared through a cloud of dust debris.
"How did you do that".
Benjamin refuses to be complimented as he still believes that the girl was setting him up. He did not approach her on this occasion. Instead he grabs her by her arm just like most girls she spends to be hurt and tells him to let go. He grabs her again pulling her she resists he continues
"You knew didn't you"
"Know what"
"You know where he is."
"No."
"You think you with me but you are way way over there."
As Lucy tries to explain herself to him. Benjamin continues.
"they will not have time to think about it the next time. I think that his gone underground the only way into that building was if it was still standing and as it happens it is now a ton of bricks."
The girl Lucy is getting upset and she wants Benjamin to believe her, Benjamin is really having a go at her.
"I mean whose side are you on. I mean come how did you ken ow that the building was going to explode."

"What, because you think that I knew that the building was going to go you think I had something to do with it."
"I have never heard so much poppycock in my entire life. The girl continues trying to preside beaming s conscious she continues.
" It was a promotion, or luck, I just knew okay. You could call it intuition.
The girl grabs Benjamin by his arm she says softly "I'm in I am one of you. I just needed a chance to get away."
Lucy begins to cry,
"I just needed someone."
"What and that someone just had to be me."
"yes you."
"We will discuss this again after we have finished our business."
She turns away
What's wrong with you now she gets behind Benjamin slowly pushing a gun into the back of his neck.
Benjamin not so surprised tells her
"you're not going to pull the trigger."
Lucy takes the gun away proving that she was on his side of things.
"Try me again some time." Lucy says as she walks away.
Benjamin continues to go after the microchip.

THE END

www.ingramcontent.com/pod-product-compliance
Ingram Content Group UK Ltd.
Pitfield, Milton Keynes, MK11 3LW, UK
UKHW041850190726
13854UKWH00002B/801

9 781788 760362